EVIL
WAKE

EVIL WAKE

Episode Three of Dr. Hardy, ME

Willoughby Hundley III, MD

EVIL WAKE
EPISODE THREE OF DR. HARDY, ME

iUniverse books may be ordered through booksellers or by contacting:

iUniverse
1663 Liberty Drive
Bloomington, IN 47403
www.iuniverse.com
1-800-Authors (1-800-288-4677)

ISBN: 978-1-5320-4503-5 (sc)
ISBN: 978-1-5320-4504-2 (hc)
ISBN: 978-1-5320-4502-8 (e)

Library of Congress Control Number: 2018904534

Print information available on the last page.

iUniverse rev. date: 04/21/2018

With greatest thanks to my wife, Lucy,
whose support made this book possible

Chapter 1

Working night duty in the ER was stressful, both physically and psychically, as keeping alert during those hours opposed the body's natural circadian rhythm. Dr. Obie Hardy, finishing his twelve-hour assignment, walked out through the ambulance bay. He squinted at the morning sunlight, glad that this was Monday and the end of his week of graveyard shifts. The warm, humid August air and his night-shift "hangover" left him feeling as if he were in a haze. During his mechanical, dream-like drive home, Hardy reflected on the fact that sleep deprivation was the equivalent of driving under the influence; it impaired perception and slowed reflexes. *I'm not getting any younger*, thought the fifty-six-year-old. He turned onto his long, rocky driveway.

After he had showered, he exchanged places with his wife, Lucy, who was still lying in bed. "Good night," he said, kissing her.

She got up and put on her housecoat. "Good night. I hope you sleep well," she said before exiting the bedroom.

When he next heard her voice three hours later, it seemed that mere minutes had passed. "Obie. You've got an ME call."

"What?" he muttered groggily.

"It's the Richmond office. There's an ME case here."

"Okay." He took the phone from her and spoke into it. "Dr. Hardy here." The investigator told him about a death scene on Greenwood Road, only about three miles from his home. Dr. Hardy was one of the four medical examiners, or MEs, in Mecklenburg County, a rural county in southside Virginia. Local

1

physicians who chose to provide the community service acted as field agents of the state's medical examiner's office.

"I can be there in ten minutes," said the sleep-deprived Hardy. He sat on the edge of the bed, letting the feeling return to his somnolent body.

"You shouldn't be driving without any decent rest," said Lucy. "I can drive you to the scene."

"Okay, great." He didn't need her to twist his arm about that. "Let's take the Jeep, though." Greenwood Road was a gravel road, and an ME case there would likely be in even more rugged terrain. In contrast to the neatly dressed brunette chauffeuse, an unshaven and T-shirt-clad Dr. Hardy set out for the scene.

Pastureland and woods bordered the gravel road, with occasional scattered, rare small homesites. No numbered street addresses existed there. Fortunately, a county police car was parked off to the left side, marking the entrance to the site. Accompanying the police car were a blue Crown Victoria and a gray van with Tanner Funeral Home painted on the side.

Lucy parked near the cruiser, and they were greeted by a county deputy. She carried a clipboard and wore white shorts and sandals. The officer led them down a tire-trodden trail into the woods. After about 150 yards, they reached the scene. Dozens of freshly dug mounds of dirt lay along four parallel rows, each marked with a small numbered flag. Idly poised nearby was a yellow backhoe machine. An occasional weathered headstone hinted that this was an ancient graveyard. Dr. Hardy was a bit bewildered.

"Our body's over toward the lake," said the deputy, directing him. Three people stood near a new digging. Dr. Hardy recognized Bruce Duffer, the six-foot-tall Mecklenburg County detective who was one of the group.

"Dr. Hardy," the detective said. "This one's a bit bizarre." Duffer was a seasoned officer in his fifties. He gestured to the blonde lady beside him. "Oh, this is Betty Tanner, from Tanner Funeral Home. She discovered the body."

"Okay," Hardy said. He was familiar with Betty since through his profession he had met most of the local morticians. He smiled at her and said, "What's up with all those graves?"

"Well," answered Betty, "the Corps has contracted me to relocate the remains in this old graveyard." The reservoir lake was managed by the US Army Corps of Engineers. "They have concerns that erosion might wash open the graves. Also, the Munsford Trail passes along here." Betty appeared about forty; she was neat and perky. "Gary, my digger, noted some red clay exposed off to this edge. When he dug some away, he found a body that appeared *fresher* than those in the other graves."

The corpse was only partially exposed with the head and back showing. The dirt and decay made an immediate determination of age and race impossible. Detective Duffer leaned over the site, clicking his camera, as Gary carefully picked away the soil with a flower-potting shovel. The remains of a T-shirt and jeans clung to the body, blackened by rot and possibly old blood. With gloved hands, Betty and Dr. Hardy began assisting Gary in unearthing the body. Duffer laid out a sheet alongside the grave and probed the body's jean pockets.

"Great! No wallet!" he said. "Are we ready to turn him over, Doc?"

"Yeah. Okay," said Hardy.

"Let's roll him onto the sheet." Gary and Betty stepped back while they carefully maneuvered the human remains onto the sheet. Facial identification was impossible, since the soft tissues of the face, the nose, eyes, and lips were dissolved from decay. The hair appeared to have been brown, and bare skull was exposed on the top of the head. Disturbing the shallow grave had intensified the fetid odor of decomposition.

"We'll need an autopsy for ID and determining the cause of death," said Dr. Hardy.

"How long do you think he's been dead?" Duffer asked.

"I'd guess three to four months." Hardy knew this was just that, a guess. It usually took about six months to completely skeletonize. "Not more than six," he continued. "The hair's short, and the clothing appears male. The postmortem may find usable DNA, but at least the pelvic bone structure can confirm the sex."

"Okay. I can start with a presumed male, probably Caucasian since the hair was brown and straight. Age?"

"Well, the teeth are in fair shape. It's doubtful that he's elderly. His age could range from thirty to sixty years."

"Fair enough. I'll start a missing persons search while we wait for the autopsy results."

"Which funeral home will take him to Richmond?" asked Hardy. "Tanner's?"

"That would be the simplest," Duffer said, looking to Betty Tanner. "Okay?"

"Sure," said Betty. "We can load him in our van now."

"I'll call the Richmond office," said Hardy. The Central Office of Medical Examiners was the regional office that covered Mecklenburg County. He got out his phone and relayed his field findings to the office investigator. Then he set the case up for autopsy in Richmond, one hundred miles to the north. Turning to Betty, he said, "You're clear to transport him to Richmond. So, what's this graveyard project you're doing here?"

"Well, we're relocating these graves. So far we've cataloged fifty-seven sites. We take the remains to the garage of my funeral home in South Hill. They're arranged on the floor with everything we uncover in the graves—personal effects, jewelry, and such. The Corps of Engineers oversees the entire project."

"Are the bodies identifiable?"

"Very few graves are marked. We assign them all numbers. Some have monogrammed items or jewelry, and we add those initials to their ID numbers, at least."

"How old are these graves?" Lucy asked, her interest apparently tweaked by the mention of jewelry.

"We've estimated they're from the mid-1800s."

"Wow!" said Lucy. "That was before the civil war!"

"Yeah. And this is a black graveyard—African American. They were all likely slaves or servants."

"This is a fascinating project," said Dr. Hardy.

"You're welcome to come by the funeral home and see what we're doing."

"I'd like that a lot," he responded.

Gary approached them, pushing a litter. He was a hefty man whose progress was little impeded by the wheels jerking roughly along the ground.

"Oh, thanks, Gary," said Betty. "We'll head up to Richmond when he's loaded."

As Gary and Betty closed the back doors of the funeral home van, a sound arose from the lake. Hardy looked out across the water, squinting into the bright reflections of sunlight. He could make out the silhouette of a solitary fishing boat about two hundred yards offshore. The drone of a small outboard motor rang out as the boat headed off, moving away from them. Duffer gazed out at the vessel as well. Most likely it was a lone fisherman seeking a more productive site.

Chapter 2

Dr. Hardy clicked his computer mouse over the ER bed 3 icon on his screen, assigning himself someone named Norton. Norton's complaint was summarized in the record as "psych." He groaned under his breath, anticipating a lengthy, rambling medical history. Pulling open the curtain shielding room 3, Dr. Hardy found Mr. Norton.

"Hello, Mr. Norton. I'm Dr. Hardy." The patient was a white male; he was sitting on the side of the litter. He spit onto the floor before answering.

"Hello, Doc." He was well tanned and wearing a white T-shirt and khaki-colored, pocketed vest. Beside him on the sheet was a tan bush hat.

"What can we help you with?"

"You know, camels can go two weeks without water."

"Yeah, I've heard that. Are you feeling okay?"

"I guess I got too hot," he said, looking up at Dr. Hardy. "They said I was acting funny." He pulled a celery stalk out of a vest pocket and bit off a piece. "It's for the camel, but we share," he informed Hardy, a smile spreading over his face.

"Well, let me just check your heart and lungs," said Hardy. The man was obviously loopy. Hardy decided to just focus on his physical condition. He donned his stethoscope and examined those areas. As he stood back up, his patient took a sip from his cup of water and spit again on the floor.

"Camels spit, you know."

Dr. Hardy felt he had obtained enough information to formulate a diagnosis and turned to leave. His foot slipped on the large puddle of Norton spittle on the tiled floor. He pulled the curtain closed and shook his head.

A county deputy stood outside the exam room, holding a leather saddlebag.

"Did you lose your mount?" asked Hardy.

"No. I just took these off the llama we have tied up outside."

"A llama?"

"Yeah. We brought in a fellow who was walking the streets with the llama. We thought he might be having a heat stroke."

"Really? A llama?" It was close to a camel.

"Yeah. He's tied up out front in the shade."

"Okay. He's in there. Oh, and watch your step. Camels spit." He would need the drug screen results before calling psychiatry. *Another routine day at the oasis*, he thought.

"Dr. Hardy," called the ER unit secretary. "The medical examiner's office is on the line."

"Okay," Hardy responded. He took the call on the cordless phone. The investigator, a female, informed him of a highway fatality that needed viewing by an ME. "I'm working in the ER until 10 pm," said Hardy.

"I'll see if the funeral home can bring the body to the hospital," said the investigator.

"That could work."

Thirty minutes later, Dr. Hardy met the funeral director outside the basement level door adjacent to the morgue. He wedged a broken brick in the doorway to avoid being locked out of the hospital. The driver's door of the hearse opened, and Betty Tanner emerged with a mild air of frustration.

"Okay," she said. "I hope you can complete your exam out here. He's *quite* large!" She opened the side door behind the driver's seat.

"Sure," said Hardy. Unlike an ambulance, the back floor of

the hearse was at a level similar to the rear of a station wagon. To access the body, he had to squat and creep inside. The decedent, Marvin Jensen, was a whale of a man. After the investigator had called, Hardy had scanned the hospital records for any possible medical history. He was diabetic and reportedly weighed 415 pounds, documented during an ER visit earlier that same day.

There was no head room for Hardy to obtain an overhead, frontal look, limiting his exam to a side view. The head had a dried blood trail from the nostrils across the right cheek. Hardy pressed in on the facial bones and felt them shifting, making a dull clunking sound.

"Head injury with facial fractures," Hardy thought aloud. "Did he hit the windshield or the steering wheel?"

"Well," said Betty. "He was thrown thirty feet from the vehicle."

"He was in the ER earlier, with a low-sugar reaction. I noticed him when he walked out, saying he was headed to McDonald's for a couple of Big Macs. I doubt this was from another hypoglycemic spell."

"And he was travelling at a high speed. He didn't make the turn," said Betty. She had picked up the body from the wreck site.

"Was he thrown through the windshield?"

"Most likely through the sunroof!"

Hardy tried to imagine the forces involved in thrusting this man up through the roof. The head trauma had indeed caused his death, making it accidental. Even if there was a remote chance that a low blood sugar had caused the crash, the hypoglycemia would not likely have been fatal.

"The manner of death is definitely accidental," Hardy concluded. "I'll need to examine the rest of the body and draw blood samples."

Betty opened the rear door for Hardy, and he climbed in on his knees. The body was mostly faceup, but it was tipped somewhat onto the right side. *Listing to starboard*, Hardy thought.

He palpated the lower extremity bones, although the thick layer of fatty tissue would conceal all but the most obvious fractures. To gain access to the groin area for blood sampling, Hardy attempted to straighten the hips. He pulled down the jeans and rolled the corpse to the left side. The obese body smothered the usual floor casket rollers, and a palette-type dolly had been wedged under the torso. When Hardy manipulated the body, the dolly slid backward, out from underneath, leaving the corpse lying on its right side.

"I can't reach the femorals," he said as he backed out of the door. "I'll have to try the subclavians." He didn't reveal that he had dislodged the dolly. Hopefully she had assistants to help her handle this "dead weight."

Finally, Dr. Hardy had his specimens but felt as if he had lost the battle of the bulge.

His exasperation must have been obvious to the funeral director. "This is one for the books!" she said.

"Yeah!" agreed Hardy. He then added, "Oh, by the way— how's the gravesite relocation going?"

"Pretty good. We've done forty-nine graves so far. We're still digging and re-entering. Why don't you stop by my garage and check it out?"

"I'd like to. Could I come in the morning before my shift?"

"Sure. I'll be there until 9 or so. After that, I'll go to the site."

"Great."

The following morning, Dr. Hardy drove over to the garage to the rear of Tanner's Funeral Home. Betty was there, along with a slender, balding man, who was holding what appeared to be a paint brush. He was kneeling beside some dark-brown objects. There were ten clusters of these items laid out upon the cement floor.

"Dr. Hardy, I'm glad you could come by," said Betty. "This is Carl. He's the archeologist working on this project."

"Hello," Carl said, mechanically. He nodded and returned to his brushing.

"Dr. Hardy's a local medical examiner," Betty informed him.

"Oh?" said Carl, now showing more enthusiasm.

"Yeah. I was at the site a couple of weeks ago," said Dr. Hardy.

"We call it site C-57," said Carl, sounding a bit nerdy. "I've been studying these bones to determine age and sex and, possibly, clues as to why these people died."

"That sounds interesting," said Hardy.

"I've found many skulls with grooves in the palates, probably indicating a bout of illness with a high fever. This most likely correlates with the worldwide influenza epidemic of 1857 to 1859. They, of course, would have been the survivors, allowing development of the bony grooves. There was also a yellow fever outbreak in the US in 1852, but it was focused more to the south of Virginia."

"Fascinating epidemiology," said Hardy.

"Some of the graves contained jewelry," said Betty. "We've traced the origin back to Yugoslavia!"

"So these people weren't just slaves?" asked Hardy.

"No. Not common slaves, anyway. Maybe house domestics or indentured servants," said Betty. "We gather the contents of each grave and place them in infant caskets to re-enter in the La Crosse Cemetery."

"The Corps of Engineers' Samuel Goode plot," said Carl. "That was the only legible name we found on the grave markers."

"I could stay here all day, but I need to get to work. Thanks for showing me some of this project," said Dr. Hardy.

"Sure," said Betty. "Oh, have you found out any more about the body we found there?"

"Well, no. It can take four to six weeks to get an ME autopsy report. The DNA is often the hang-up."

"You mean an archaeologist's work moves faster than the medical examiner's?" asked Carl, with a hint of excitement.

"Oddly enough, it does!"

Another two weeks passed before Dr. Hardy received the autopsy report for the lakeside grave case. The yellow-colored pages reported that the body had been ID'd as Victor Soloman, a thirty-seven-year-old white male. April was the estimated time of death, making the corpse four months old. The toxicologies were of little use, as the only compounds that could survive decomposition were the heavy metals such as lead, arsenic, and mercury. None of these had been discovered. The shirt showed bloodstains and three apparent knife holes. The cause of death was exsanguination from multiple stab wounds—and the manner of death was ruled homicide.

The stab wounds are a bit circumstantial, thought Hardy. The skin was deteriorated, even to the point of the skull being exposed. *Wouldn't the hair have protected the scalp and slowed its decomposition?* he thought. Animal pelts were used by primitive cultures for months or years. Further scrutinizing the report, he saw that a scalping injury to the head was described, apparently a perimortem wound.

"A scalping?" he wondered aloud.

Chapter 3

Detective Bruce Duffer was sitting at his metal desk in the Mecklenburg County sheriff's office when he opened his envelope from the ME's office. He welcomed the break from pursuing a cold case, sixty-five years old. Murders have no statute of limitations, and unsolved cases can linger for decades. This one was a triple murder, the Garner brothers, so it was actually three cases in one. Apparently, it had occurred during a vicious robbery, about a decade after the nation had emerged from the Great Depression. He had been unsuccessful in discovering a fresh angle on the investigation.

He pushed aside the cardboard box of files to focus on this most recent postmortem report. The physical features of the body had matched that of three local missing persons. Victor Soloman's definitive ID had been confirmed by a DNA match through CODIS. CODIS—Combined DNA Index System—was the FBI database of logged DNA. Despite such modern technology, 23 percent of unidentified human remains remained unknown. This, at least, was a positive start for this case. Duffer studied the report; apparently this had been a stabbing victim. Duffer was taken aback by the description of the head wound.

"A scalping?" he said to himself. "Why?" This had been a brutal murder! He pushed the call button on his desk phone for the clerk. "Betsy," he said.

"Yes, Detective Duffer," was his answer.

"Can you pull me the file on the missing person Victor Soloman, please?"

"Sure thing."

Betsy soon entered Duffer's office with a manila folder. "I'm surprised we haven't e-filed this one yet," she said. "It's been almost five months."

"A missing person often becomes a murder," Duffer explained. "We keep hard files for up to twenty years, in case a body turns up."

"I take it that you have a body now."

"Definitely!" He held up the autopsy report.

Scrutinizing the Soloman file, Duffer hoped to find a motive or a clue to help launch the investigation. The man's car and trailer had been found at the Eastland Creek boat ramp. His boat had been discovered beached about a half mile away. The life jackets, fishing gear, and some sonar equipment had been missing from the vessel. The man had been a thirty-four-year-old insurance salesman from two counties away who was visiting the lake to fish for bass. The violence of this homicide seemed disproportionately severe for a petty theft. The loot was valued at less than $1,000. There had to be a more diabolical motive.

The postmortem exam had revealed no additional clues. Opening it up to the public might elicit some tips. He called to Betsy again.

"Can you get me the *News Progress* reporter on the line?" he said.

"Sure," she answered. Half an hour passed before the newsman returned their call.

"This is Mark McClain from the *News Progress*," he announced.

"Good," said Duffer. He knew McClain and trusted that the article would be done well. "We've ID'd the body of a murdered person and need help to bring in some tips from the public."

"No problem. So, give me the scoop."

Duffer recanted the case, from missing person, to fishing boat, to lakeside grave. He purposefully omitted the detail of the scalp injury. It would not be helpful for the general population to know this, and it could possibly instill fear or panic.

"Oh," he added. "Can you see if Soloman's local paper can run the story too? Someone from his home may be aware of a conflict or other useful information."

"Yeah, sure. I can release it to the *Richmond Times Leader* as well. I hope you get some leads. Can I get a photo to run with it?"

"Will do. And thanks again."

So, this five month-old case, a gruesome murder with no clear motive, was getting off to a slow start. A uniformed man with a mustache looked in Duffer's doorway, interrupting his train of thought.

"Hey, Bruce," he said.

"What's up, Tom?" said Duffer, addressing the county dog warden. His official title was the animal control officer. "Rounding up strays?"

"I wish. No, I just loaded up a full-grown doe killed near Beechwood Point." Their rural county had an estimated deer population of twenty-five thousand, only about seven thousand less than that of humans. Vehicular accidents with deer were not uncommon. "And it's still two months before hunting season."

"Anyone hurt?" asked Duffer.

"Nope. Just a hit and run." He smiled at Duffer and continued on down the hall.

Chapter 4

Dr. Hardy drove along Taylor Ferry Road, outside of Boydton, heading home. He disliked the mid shift assignment in the ER because it put him so late getting home. It was dark along the country road at eleven at night, and his eyes were tired after the twelve-hour workday. The solitude and peacefulness of rural life brought with it an abundance of wildlife. Consequently, Hardy was always vigilant for deer, but he hardly caught a glimpse of the small mammal crouched in the ditch. A flash of white fur splotched with black and tan markings darted out into the road. Hardy stomped on the brake but groaned when he felt the sickening thud of the impact.

"Crap!" he exclaimed. Looking into the rearview, he saw only empty road—no sign of the cat carcass. It was late, and dark, and there was no way that the cat could have survived that solid a hit. He believed the body must have fallen back into the ditch. His driveway entrance was just a few yards ahead.

"I'll call Mrs. Davis in the morning," he spoke aloud. She lived about a quarter of a mile back and had a number of outdoor cats. *It had to be one of her clowder,* he thought. Downtrodden, he proceeded slowly, turning into his driveway.

"I killed a cat near the driveway," he confessed to Lucy once inside.

"Aw!" she said. "Probably one of Mrs. Davis's."

"Yeah, probably. I'll look for the body in the morning and give her a call."

The following morning, Dr. Hardy left a little early to check the scene. He parked and searched the pavement. There was no blood or fur. The ditches were empty, except for a double-deuce beer can and a Styrofoam cup.

That's strange, he thought. Feeling guilty, he phoned Mrs. Davis anyway. She reported that none of her cats were missing. As Dr. Hardy resumed his commute to work, he assured himself that he hadn't imagined the incident.

Driving through town, Hardy stopped by the convenience store for a couple of Diet Sun Drop drinks for his workday caffeine fix. He continued east out of town and noticed a new business sign up for the car wash at the Wilson Street intersection. Before, there had just been a few guys playing the radio and scrubbing automobiles on that street corner. Now, JB's Car Wash was the automobile enhancement establishment of Boydton. Hardy knew the man of "JB" namesake—Jerome Benjamin Tyler. JB was well known in the community and had done various odd jobs, from custodial services for the county offices to lawn care. This marked his official plunge into the business world.

JB was a cheerful black man in his midthirties, whose thin mustache accented his omnipresent smile. He seemed to enjoy life, whether at work or play. He lived on Skipwith Road, in a small house with a neatly groomed yard, a reflection of the propensity for tidiness that flowed over into his car-care enterprise. His own car was a red SUV, and as a single man, he enjoyed a certain popularity with the ladies.

Great! Dr. Hardy thought after passing the new sign. *Maybe I'll get my Jeep cleaned up.*

Once at work in the ER, Dr. Hardy began sorting through the variety of ailments presenting to him, from a toothache to a vaginal discharge. Suddenly, two EMTs from South Hill Rescue entered through the ambulance doors, escorting an injured black male. One EMT, in an orange uniform T-shirt with EMT in large white print on the back, began reporting. "This thirty-eight-year-old male was assaulted at 12:30 with fists and beer bottles to the head. No loss of consciousness but multiple facial and scalp wounds. He refused to lie on the stretcher." His patient was walking with a slow but steady gait. White gauze was wrapped about his head. Crusted and wet dark-burgundy blood formed streaks down his face. "Glascow Coma 15," concluded the EMT. This was the scale they used to assess level of consciousness in patients.

"Thanks," Dr. Hardy said as a nurse placed the patient in the trauma 1 bay. Wishing to establish that the patient's cognitive functions were indeed intact, Hardy addressed the patient. "What's your name, sir?"

"Ah, Roger Lewis," the patient said.

Patent airway, normal speech, thought Hardy. "Where are we now?"

"The South Hill ER."

Good. He's oriented. "Let's get his vitals," said Hardy, although he saw that two nurses were already performing that task. "I'm going to unwrap his head and assess these wounds. Does your head hurt, sir?"

"Yeah, some."

As Dr. Hardy peeled off the gauze, he found a cut over the left eyebrow, another at the forehead scalp line, and a large gash in the back of the head. It was a flap of skin from which blood was pumping with his pulse.

An incomplete scalping! thought Hardy. "Okay, I'll need a suture tray to ligate these bleeders," he said. Before this preparation could be made, Roger Lewis's body tensed up, and he made some grunting like sounds. Immediately, he began convulsing with his head and extremities. With the head wounds now open, the jerky seizure activity splashed gushing blood in all directions, spraying the walls, exam litter, curtains, and ER staff with the red rain. Dr. Hardy was stunned momentarily before he reached for a personal protective gear pack.

After two minutes, the seizing and blood shower abated enough that the now garbed ER staff could safely return to the bedside.

"Let's get an IV," called the brunette nurse who was grabbing an arm. "Some Ativan?" she asked Dr. Hardy.

"Yes," said Dr. Hardy, trying to regain his composure. "One milligram of lorazepam IV." The internal head injury was worse than he had expected. They needed an immediate CT scan of the head. "We'll need to intubate him and keep him sedated for the head CT."

"Are you planning to keep him here?" asked the nurse.

"No. We'll stabilize him and transfer him to neurosurgery," said Hardy.

Trauma One looked like a crime scene, with blood spattered everywhere. When the paramedics left with Lewis for the Air Evac chopper, Dr. Hardy felt wasted. Seven hours still remained in his shift. He felt as if he had been in a horror movie. The Victor Soloman case with the scalping wound came to mind. Could that murder have been as gruesome as this had been?

Chapter 5

Jerome Benjamin was on the job at the car wash. A county police cruiser pulled up and stopped just long enough for Detective Bruce Duffer to emerge from the passenger door. The car pulled away as Duffer approached.

"Detective Duffer," JB greeted him. "We've finished your car." He motioned toward the pale-blue Crown Victoria sedan on his lot. "She's not new, but she's clean!"

"Yep. It looks a lot better. Thanks, JB," said Duffer. He handed JB three dollars. "Here. This is for you. The office will cover the wash job."

"Sure. Thanks!"

As the detective drove off, a dingy, bronze-colored Chevrolet pickup came onto the car wash lot. A tall, hefty, dark-haired man in his late thirties stepped out of the vehicle. His tan-colored skin was weathered, stained by a combination of sun exposure and uncleanliness. Opening the passenger door, he lifted out a cardboard box and carried it toward JB. The carton had Glistex printed on its side.

"Wayne," said JB. "How are you doing?"

"Ah right," Wayne Dodson said, grinning. "Got ya a case of 'soap.'"

"Good. Let's put it inside." JB looked around as he walked through the open bay of the blue aluminum garage building. He opened the storage closet door and said, "Set it in here."

"It's your usual order," said Dodson, dropping the box roughly on the floor. JB produced a roll of bills from his pants pocket and peeled off a number of tens and twenties.

"Two fifty?" he said.

"That's right," said Dodson, taking the cash. "I'll check with you next week."

"That'll be great. Thanks!" JB watched the truck drive off. Something about Wayne just made him feel creepy. JB's crew had begun wetting down a black SUV as a middle-aged man stood nearby watching. JB approached him. "Is that one yours?" he asked.

"Yeah. I hit a damned deer yesterday evening," he said.

"Oh. I'm sorry to hear it. Did it do much damage?"

"Naw. Just a little dent and a busted headlight. I got a new light, but the deer shit all over my hood!"

"I can see why you need JB's!"

"It was the damnedest thing, though. He looked like he was staggering, not scared at all when I hit him. And in broad daylight!"

"That's just crazy. We'll clean you up good, okay?" JB patted him on his shoulder.

"Yeah, thanks!"

With his clean vehicle parked outside the county sheriff's office, Detective Duffer went in and surveyed the folders of paperwork on his desk. He had hoped for a lead in the Soloman murder, but there were no new developments. The box with the Garner brothers cold case killings caught his eye. This was not a mere unsolved crime; it had become local folklore. Almost everyone in the community had heard the story told, embellished with conjectures as to who the perpetrators were. Duffer held somewhat of a vendetta to solve this famous mystery. He picked up the black-and-white photos from the 1950 scene. The bodies each had a dozen stab wounds. Pictures taken outside showed that small holes had been dug in the yard. Friends and neighbors claimed the Garners had mistrusted the banks, a position fostered by having been raised during the Depression. Consequently, they were rumored to have buried their money in jars for security.

FDIC: Funds Deposited in Containers, thought Duffer with a smile. That was the Garners' version of the banks' Federal Deposit Insurance Corporation. The dirt-caked empty jars found at the scene implied that a successful robbery had been the motive for the murders. No murder weapon had been recovered. The glass jars had yielded no clean fingerprints, leaving the case with no hard evidence. A bloodstained handkerchief had tested positive only for the victim's blood. Duffer looked at the photo of the handkerchief, an essential accessory item for men in days past, now fallen into disuse, much like the cloth diaper. The bloodstains were obvious. He also noticed, however, a smeared area of soil near the center. Most likely it was nasal secretions—snot.

"Hey!" he said aloud, and then he pushed his phone intercom button. "Betsy. Can you get me an evidence item from the Garner case?"

"Sure, Detective Duffer. Which item do you need?"

"Item 12, the handkerchief."

"Okay. I'll see if I can locate it."

"Thanks!" There had been no DNA testing ability in 1950. The handkerchief could contain body fluid from the killer. It was a long shot, but at least it was a possible clue in this legendary mystery.

Chapter 6

Dusk was fast approaching under overcast skies as Dr. Hardy drove toward the dam. The temperature was in the upper fifties and falling, giving rise to a light fog over the ponds and creeks along the roadside where the waters retained some of the day's warmth. Early November in southern Virginia commonly brought mild weather so that fishing season remained fruitful well into the fall. Hardy assumed this ME call would be an accidental drowning of a fisherman. He turned into the parking area on the downstream side of Kerr Dam. Parking lights from an ambulance, a blue Crown Victoria, and an SUV trailering a boat brightened the graveled lot. Detective Duffer greeted him by handing him a pair of blue rubber gloves.

"This one's a doozy, Dr. Hardy." He led Hardy over to the aluminum boat beached at the water's edge.

"A fisherman?" asked Hardy.

"Well, technically, yes." He pulled back the sheet in the boat and exposed the corpse. "But not a drowning." The body was bloated from submersion, the bald head atop a face so swollen that most of the features were obscured. There were numerous cuts in his shirt, corresponded to wounds covering his torso.

"My God! He looks like a pincushion!" said Hardy. There was a pungent, rotten odor; its intensity, having been dampened by the cool water, was now released into the open air.

"Yep. He's been down five days. And someone wanted him to stay down." Duffer tugged on the ropes tied around his ankles, showing the railroad spikes attached as anchors. "He was in eight feet of water when someone spotted something along the surface. The lake's pretty shallow along this stretch."

"Do you know who this is?"

"Well, presumed to be Vance Kort. He's been missing five days. His vehicle was found parked up there." Duffer pointed toward the dam, a common gathering site for striper fishing. "He's a forty-two-year-old from Tidewater. Apparently, he was here fishing at night."

"At night? Fishing?"

"Oh yeah! They're hard-core fishermen here, 24/7 in season."

Dr. Hardy focused his attention on the body. The facial swelling hid any details, and palpation revealed no obvious fractures. The trunk was riddled with dozens of stab wounds. The corpse had on jeans and boots, and Hardy ascertained no skeletal damage. He estimated the man's height to be six feet and weight approximately two hundred pounds, difficult to assess after submersion and bloating.

"This one's for Richmond," said Hardy. "He definitely needs a postmortem. The manner of death appears to be homicide."

"Does the time of death seem consistent with the time frame?" asked Duffer.

"Yeah, I think so. Who'll take him to Richmond?"

"I've called Draper's Funeral Home from South Hill. They'll transport the body."

It was nearly midnight when the Draper's Funeral Home van arrived at the Office of the Central Medical Examiner (OCME) in Richmond. Randy, the driver, had called ahead to ensure that someone would be awaiting the delivery. He backed the van up to the loading bay and rang the doorbell. The autumn night had chilled the air to forty-five degrees, and random puffs of wind forced the cold through his clothing. He rang the bell again, rubbing his hands together to warm them. The metal door scraped open, and a voice called out. "All right! All right! What ya got there?" A black man about forty years old appeared in the doorway.

"Draper's Funeral Home. Body from Mecklenburg County."

"Okay. Just a minute." The door thumped closed as a motor began whining, raising the garage-type door. "Bring it on in."

Randy opened the van's back door and wrestled the loaded stretcher out. He lifted the leading end onto the concrete bay deck, pulled it forward and, when the rear wheels were on the stoop, began pushing the heavy cot through the doorway. The doorman waited, standing idly beside an above-the-waist height stretcher in the hallway. Since the body was from an ME case in the field, Randy had used an old litter that sat only twelve inches above the floor. He dared not risk damaging his expensive hydraulic lift on a call in the bush. This litter could be raised manually with an attendant on either side, if it didn't get jammed.

"Hey, buddy. Can you give me a hand lifting the stretcher?" asked Randy.

The doorman appeared to be an able-bodied, stout man. His size made one and a half of Randy's. "No. My job prohibits me from lifting."

"Really?" He was, needless to say, the night doorman receiving bodies for autopsy. "I can't get him up there by myself," Randy said.

"Sorry, but I can't do it." His eyes were unsympathetic.

"How about if I give you ten bucks to help me out?"

"No. Uh-uh." The doorman shook his head.

"You're serious? I told you I can't lift this body by myself." He had already struggled to unload it and wheeled it into the hallway without any offered assistance.

"I've been ordered not to do it. My job description and all."

Their gazes met in an unwavering stare. Randy shrugged and broke the brief silence.

"Okay, buddy," he said, lifting one side of the cart. The body, encased in the white vinyl body bag, rolled off onto the floor. "He's all yours!" A small puddle formed as water seeped through the zippered seam.

Randy retreated to the van with his empty cot, loaded it in the back, and slammed the door closed. As he cranked up the vehicle, the doorman called out to him. "Hey! You can't leave this here on the floor! Whatta ya doing?"

"Sorry, bud," Randy called back through the driver's window as he drove off. "It's not in *my* job description!"

Chapter 7

"I can't believe it!" said Lucy Hardy as she burst through the door from the garage. "I hit a cat near the same place you did!"

Dr. Hardy was using his computer pad at the kitchen bar area. "Really? That's strange."

"It just scooched out in front of me!"

"What did it look like?"

"I'm not sure," said Lucy. "It was so quick. White, maybe, with some spots."

"Just like the one I hit!" said Hardy.

"Well, I guess you didn't kill it, then. It looks like it would have learned its lesson and kept out of the road." It was early evening now.

"I'll check for it in the morning."

"I know it's dead. I felt the thump."

The following morning, Dr. Hardy stopped near the driveway entrance and walked the ditches for a hundred yards or so. He recalled his previous fruitless search. This morning, again, he found no cat, no blood, and no buzzards circling above. He didn't wish to appear foolish again, so he refrained from phoning anyone and drove on to the hospital for his shift.

At work, Dr. Hardy read the complaint of his first patient from his computer screen: "Swollen feet and high blood pressure." The case appeared straightforward, and he headed off to the exam bay.

"Mr. Faulk? I'm Dr. Hardy. How can we help you today?"

"Well, doc," the man replied, "my liver's bad." Mr. Faulk was an overweight white male with obvious scratches scattered over his skin. Some had scabs, and others appeared wet. "You know," he said, holding up his arms, "you can see the wastes coming out in my sores. And I'm all swole up. They say it's six roaches of the liver."

Dr. Hardy mentally translated the quite descriptive history. Faulk had *cirrhosis* of the liver, which caused fluid buildup in the abdomen—ascites. This led to edema in the lower body. The bilirubin, a waste product of liver metabolism, would accumulate and cause skin itching, leading to open scratch wounds.

"Do you drink alcohol?" asked Dr. Hardy.

"Not anymore. You see, I saw them murder someone. I was afraid I'd be next."

"A murder?"

"Yeah, but they left no trace of him. They took us to Red Lobster for his last meal. We boozed it up a little. Then, they took us down to the river. They showed us a treasure chest, washed up on a sandbar." His eyes sparkled as he told his tale. "There were some inner tubes on the beach. They told us to get in the inner tubes and swim out to the treasure chest. I said no and waited by the car. The other guy didn't see the alligators waiting in the water." Faulk raised his eyebrows, and a slight smile crossed his face.

"Well, I'll get some blood tests, check out your liver." Maybe the bilirubin level was high enough to make Mr. Faulk encephalopathic or delirious. But his story, however bizarre, was well organized, not typical of encephalopathy. High ammonia levels, another liver disease complication, usually caused sedation-like symptoms.

"You gonna check my 'Blue Ribbon'?"

"Yeah."

As Dr. Hardy walked away from the exam area, the ER nurse asked him, jokingly, "Do you want me to notify homicide?"

Dr. Hardy shook his head. "Detective Duffer won't take the case. The alligators, remember? No body!"

At the sheriff's office, Detective Duffer sat at his desk, perusing the Vance Kort murder story in the *News Progress*. The details had been watered down appropriately to prevent disclosure of any sensitive information that could hamper the investigation. It had made front page, sharing the position with the announcement of Sheriff Clay Larrimore's retirement. The man's tall physique, western-style hat, and pipe had become iconic during his thirty years as sheriff. Deputy Skyler Daniels had been his assistant for the past four years and was favored as his replacement. Duffer shook his head, thinking the young Skyler was too inexperienced to make a competent sheriff. Personally, Duffer enjoyed the field work and could not picture himself happy at such a desk job. Maybe another candidate would arise before the election.

The DNA testing had finally returned on the Garner case handkerchief. The brown spot had yielded a DNA profile. Although this was hard evidence, it would dangle as a loose end unless there was a suspect's sample for comparison.

"Betsy," he spoke into his intercom.

"Yes?"

"Can you post the Garner case DNA profile in CODIS for me?" Since CODIS hadn't existed before 1998, it would be a needle-in-a-haystack search. But maybe the perpetrator had been young and had committed a more recent crime as well.

"Sure. I'll do it today," said Betty.

"Thanks!"

At the car wash, JB's worker, Al, found JB in the garage area.

"JB. There's a guy here that says he has twenty bucks, and he's asking for the *go green special*. What do I do?"

"It's an environmentally friendly interior detailing. I'll do it," said JB. Al nodded and walked out. JB smiled, picked up his detailing tray, and reached into the Glistex cleaner box. He placed two small plastic bags with leafy contents into his tray. As he cleaned the interior of the white coupe, he slipped the two bags into the glove compartment, exchanging them for the twenty-five dollar payment that had been left inside. JB kept this enterprise hidden from his coworkers, even though a bit of curiosity could disclose the contraband contents of the Glistex box. Anyway, the less known, the better for all. He had fewer calls for "dry powder" interior cleanings than the popular "go green specials." Hopefully, his low-volume dry powders would not draw undue attention to these cocaine transactions.

Chapter 8

It was Saturday, the week before Thanksgiving, and the trees had lost most of their colored foliage. Dr. Hardy was making good use of his weekend off by riding around the yard on his mower. Hardy used his riding mower to mulch the leaf blanket covering his backyard. He would still need to rake up some of the thickest areas, but he hoped the shredded organic debris would help build topsoil over the red clay base. His cell phone vibrated in his pocket, abruptly halting his chore. "Hello. It's Dr. Hardy."

"This is investigator Parker at the medical examiner's office. Would you be available for a scene visit?"

"Sure. Where is it?"

"Red Lawn Road out of Boydton. An apparent murder-suicide."

"I'll be there in fifteen to twenty minutes."

Dr. Hardy garaged the mower and went inside to grab his ME bag from the study. He felt that his yard work clothes would be appropriate attire, since he anticipated that the scene might well be a bit dirty.

"What are you doing?" asked Lucy.

"An ME case. A murder-suicide."

"Oh! Well ... I could help you, if you like." A murder-suicide meant there were two bodies. He could use her assistance taking notes and collecting data.

"Yeah, sure!"

Hardy drove them to the address the investigator had given him. A tan van with a sheriff's star badge on the side marked

37

the location. Detective Duffer's Crown Victoria and a county police cruiser were parked there as well. The residence was a neat-appearing mobile home with a gravel driveway. Detective Duffer was standing between the opened rear doors of the van, holding a shotgun in his blue gloved hands.

"Dr. Hardy," he said in welcome. "Twelve-gauge Browning. One of the guns used." Duffer slid the weapon into a clear plastic bag and laid it in the van.

"What's this van?" asked Hardy. "Are you CSI now?"

"CIU. Crime Investigation Unit. We use it in our more complicated cases."

"Okay. Neat. So, what's the story?"

"Come on in." He glanced at Lucy. "I'm sorry, but I can only let the doc in. We're still working the scene."

"Okay. Sure," said Dr. Hardy.

"I'll just wait here by the van," said Lucy. "I'll be a CIU nurse."

When they reached the front door, Duffer put paper booties on over his shoes and handed Dr. Hardy a pair. Hardy, having gloved up already, donned the shoe covers.

"The victims were living together here," began Duffer. "Their last known contacts were yesterday. The family called us when they found the house locked with the vehicles at home and no one answering their phones." He opened the door and led Dr. Hardy inside, pointing to the left as they entered. "This is what we found."

There was a man's body seated in a cushioned chair—with the top of his head completely missing! The base of the skull showed the smooth, cupped bed where the brain would rest, but it was devoid of scalp, cranium, or brain.

"My God!" exclaimed Hardy. Blood and tissue particles were sprayed up the wall and onto the ceiling. Off to the right of the door, the fairly intact brain rested on the floor. Hardy noted the paw prints of a cat around the organ.

"It seems the cat has nibbled at it some," stated Duffer. "The girl's over there."

Hardy looked across the living room and saw a female body sitting in another chair, not appearing maimed, looking as if she were sleeping. There was a rifle resting between her legs. Another officer, already in the room, reached down and removed the firearm.

"Rachel Avery," said Duffer. "She had a history of depression. Drank a lot on weekends. Her family reported that she wanted to leave him."

Dr. Hardy approached her first, stepping carefully to avoid debris on the floor. The floor was littered with fragments of skin, bone, and blood. The second officer, Wilt Clayton, was labeling each with a numbered square tag.

"Wilt," said Duffer. "I've started a grid. Measure perpendicular from the kitchen wall and the front wall."

As the grid vectors were plotted and photographed, Dr. Hardy examined Ms. Avery. She appeared around thirty, with dark hair, and was not unattractive. He placed his thermometer in her armpit to obtain a temp. There was full body rigor present, indicating that she had been dead at least ten to twelve hours. Dried blood streaks trailed from her scalp down to her jaw. Tracing this upstream revealed a bullet wound in the back of her head on the right.

"So, does it look like she was shot in the right side of her head?" asked Dr. Hardy.

"That's what we found," said Duffer.

"But the rifle is between her knees," said Hardy, retrieving the thermometer.

"Yeah. It doesn't look like she could have shot herself there."

"Temperature is seventy-four," stated Dr. Hardy. "With this advanced rigor and heat loss, she's probably been dead twelve hours or more."

"We'll check her hands for gunpowder residue," said Wilt.

"The other odd thing is this," said Duffer. "There's a pellet pattern in the middle of the ceiling, with shotgun wadding. His fatal shot was over there against the wall. There're also drops of blood trailing through the kitchen to the back toilet. Did he kill her and then walk back to the bedroom to get a second firearm? Did he attempt suicide unsuccessfully, shoot the ceiling, and dribble his own blood while going back to get a reload?"

"Maybe the blood-dropping sample analysis will help with that," said Wilt.

Dr. Hardy turned his attention to the male victim. The lower face was still attached but split apart and flopping forward. His right eye was still seated in the facial flab, staring blankly at the floor. *Gray eyes, brown hair*, thought Dr. Hardy, mentally noting items for his CME-1 report form. He placed his thermometer in the decedent's armpit, noting rigor stiffness of his elbows but not his hands. *He hasn't been dead as long as Rachel*, he thought. "His temp is 85.4," he said. "Rachel died hours before he did, probably four to six hours."

"That could mean this is a double suicide," said Duffer. "Unless it's a murder-suicide, staged to look like a suicide."

Seeing the top of the man's head blown off stirred Dr. Hardy's memories of the scalping case from three months back. As they walked out to the crime van, he spoke. "Oh, have you found out anything more on that scalping body?"

"The Soloman case? No. No real leads yet."

"That stabbed body from the lake was right brutal as well," said Hardy. "At least he wasn't scalped too!"

"Yeah. But he was bald. No trophy for the killer."

"That's right! Still, a shitload of stabbings."

"There were 131 stab wounds! The ME's office thinks the murderer was trying to keep the body submerged. Maybe he hoped the bloating gas would just seep out through the holes."

"That's just revolting!" Hardy was shaking his head in disgust when they reached Lucy where she was standing beside the Crime Investigation Unit.

"I got the demographics from Wilt Clayton," Lucy said.

"Great," said Dr. Hardy. He turned back to Duffer. "I'll get these forms faxed to Richmond before the autopsies."

"Very good. You two take care." Duffer returned to the house to finish processing the scene.

By the time the detectives had finished collecting their scene evidence, Duffer felt fatigued, but he was also unnerved by the horror they had found. To help unwind the tension, he took a slight detour home. He drove toward the dam and turned down Mays Chapel Road. This route carried him past the old Garner brothers' homestead. The house had been vacant for decades now. For a while some local farmers had used the building as a barn to store bales of hay. Now that baling hay into rolls had become the standard for hay storage, the house was vacant again. The grounds around the wood-frame house were overgrown with weeds and tree saplings. Duffer slowed down, looking over the area. His interest had been aroused by his recent work on this cold case. He didn't expect any revelations or clues to arise, just something to pull his mind away from the day's carnage. An old tobacco barn stood off at a distance behind the home. The barn was a log-and-cement building with a tin roof, in contrast to the modern metal barns that used propane gas heaters to cure the crops. Turning his attention back to the road, he suddenly did a double take. Was he imagining smoke coming from the tobacco barn? A faint gray haze appeared to be rising from behind the barn. "Probably someone burning leaves," he told himself aloud and continued his drive back to town.

Chapter 9

Castle Heights was little more than an intersection along Route 4, about a mile from the Buggs Island Dam. During the construction of the dam in the early fifties, it had been a bustling town. The name had arisen from the US Army Corps of Engineers' insignia, a castle. Now it was reduced to a small community where a pizzeria, a convenience store, and a bar were clustered. The bar, Castle Heights Lounge, was a gray cinder-block building with a burgundy awning on the front. It was only open on evenings of weekends and holiday Mondays. The nearby Corps of Engineers campgrounds prohibited alcohol use, so "the Castle" was a popular seasonal watering ground. In late autumn, it served predominantly local patrons, predominantly single.

Inside the Castle, JB recognized the perky blonde at the bar from a few weeks ago. She was standing there with a female friend. Her black leather-like pants and boots were sleek and sexy. He was drawn by her to the bar but, on his way over, had no idea what to say.

"Hi there," was his greeting. "Nice pants!"

She studied him briefly and took a sip of her wine cooler. He was neat and sharply dressed. Smiling, she answered, "Thanks."

"I saw you here a couple of weeks ago. I was hoping I'd get to speak to you."

"Budweiser, JB?" asked the bartender, familiar with the tastes of a regular customer.

"Yeah. Thanks."

"JB?" said the blonde. "Like the car wash?" She and her friend giggled.

"Yep. I'm the cleanup man. And you?"

"I'm Katie, and this is Jill."

"Hi, Katie and Jill."

"Hi," Jill injected.

"And what do you girls do when you're not drinking wine coolers?"

"I work at Farmers Bank in Chase City," said Katie.

"I'm at the county court building," added Jill.

As they drank at the bar, Katie's actions grew more coquettish, and JB became infatuated. This unlikely pair seemed to be hitting it off. They stepped off to dance while Jill retreated to a table with a male acquaintance. After a few dances, they joined Jill and company at their table. The evening grew late.

"I'd like to see you again sometime," JB said.

"Okay. I'll probably be here again next week. Here's my cell number." She entered it into his phone.

"Great! I can't wait."

After a week of suggestive texting, they met again at the Castle. His sexual tension had heightened from the digital foreplay, and his inhibitions had been lowered by a little alcohol.

"I'd like to show you my place," said JB.

"Well, that might be nice," she said, a bit coy.

"Did you drive here?"

"No. Jill dropped me off."

"All right. Let's go, then!" As she smiled and stood up, he took her hand. He led her to his red SUV and they drove out of the parking lot.

As they were leaving the Castle, she said, "Oh, did I tell you my dad's a deputy?"

"No, I'm sure you didn't." He had always tried to be in good standing with the law. This was probably not a big deal, and anyway, at this point libido was overpowering prudence. "That shouldn't matter," he said, almost as if it were a question.

"Nope. Not by me." She squeezed his hand but he felt only a little bit comforted.

Parked across the street from the Castle Heights Lounge was a county police cruiser. Its engine started, and it rolled out onto the highway, following the red SUV.

On Thanksgiving Day, Dr. Hardy's ER shift ended at seven in the evening, delaying his holiday meal until nearly eight. He arrived home to find his family gathered and famished. The aroma of freshly baked rolls and candied yams overpowered the turkey and cornbread dressing. A fire flickered in the dining room fireplace, beckoning the diners.

"I'm sorry to keep everybody waiting," he said.

"That's okay," said Lucy. "You're not the last to arrive. The kids have been fed, and we're still waiting on *your* daughter!"

"That would be Vikki," he guessed. She was a bit eccentric and was not known for being punctual.

"You can carve the turkey while we get everything set out."

"Okay, sure. How about a glass of wine?"

"Sure." She handed him a knife and a wine glass. Hardy had barely finished slicing the main entrée when the front door burst open. Vikki rushed in, clad in a short polka-dotted skirt and black leggings. Her sweater was embroidered with a Hello Kitty pattern.

"Oh my God!" she exclaimed. "I just hit a cat coming in! I know I killed it!" A cat owner herself, she looked horrified, with eyes watering.

"Where did it happen?" asked Dr. Hardy.

"Out near the driveway." She was unable to hold back her tears.

"What color was it?" asked Lucy.

"Mostly white, with some spots."

"Did you see the cat's body after you hit it?" asked Hardy.

"No. I glanced in the rearview, but I couldn't look back! It was dark, anyway. I don't think I can drive back by there." Lucy gave her a hug. Dr. Hardy poured her a glass of Merlot, her favorite wine, and handed it to her.

"Don't worry, Vikki," said Lucy, comforting her. "We've both hit that cat. There's never any body found, and it just shows up again later!"

"Yep. The ghost cat!" Hardy added.

Vikki looked a little relieved. Maybe it was just the comfort of her family. Maybe it was the wine kicking in. "Do you think it's that thing about having nine lives?" she asked.

"I don't know," said Hardy. "If so, three down, six to go."

"Let's eat!" commanded Lucy.

Chapter 10

Wayne Dodson followed JB into the car wash building, carrying a box of Glistex cleanser. JB took the package from him, set it on the floor, and handed him an empty Glistex box in exchange.

"You're supplying me with a quality product," said JB. "I've had good feedback."

"Good," responded Wayne, almost as a grunt.

"What's your secret?" JB handed him an envelope of cash.

"Curing." JB held his gaze, open for some elaboration. "I use a flue-curing tobacco barn." This gave his weed the same processing that commercial southside Virginia tobacco products had. This was prime quality leaf. He cracked a thin smile as he stuffed the envelope in his pocket.

"Excellent, man! Keep up the good work." JB patted Wayne's back as he walked back to his bronze pickup truck with him.

The fall season was bringing cooler weather and slower business for the car wash. It was a good time for JB to get away some, and he had arranged a Christmas shopping excursion to Southpark, in Colonial Heights, with Katie. The area had a mall and several large chain stores, including Kohl's, Target, Walmart, and Sam's. JB had booked them a room at the Hampton Inn for the night. They started at the mall and continued on to surrounding stores. Their last stop before dinner was Priscilla's, a lingerie and intimacy boutique.

"I thought stopping here might build up our appetites," said JB as they entered.

"Maybe for you," said Katie, smiling. "But I could go for some linguine and wine." She was dressed fairly sexily already.

"All right. Humor me, then, and we'll hit the Olive Garden."

"Okay. I'll just pretend I'm preparing us dessert." She held up a package of red edible panties. "How about strawberry?" she said teasingly.

"Maybe. I guess it's just the season's spirit, but I have a taste for something in stockings."

"How about this?" She held up to her body a red satin bustier with garters.

"Oh yeah!"

"I'll pick out some stockings to go with it."

JB kept his word, and they dined at the Italian restaurant. They talked, eating slowly, savoring their meal and the better part of two bottles of a domestic Zinfandel.

"We can shop a little longer if you like," JB offered.

"No, I don't think so. The stores will be even more crowded at night." She appeared relaxed and mellow after the food and wine. "Anyway, I think we have dessert waiting in the room." She smiled seductively and touched his leg with her toe under the table.

At the hotel, JB waited in anxious anticipation while Katie retreated to the bathroom with her Priscilla's bag. He selected a station on the bedside clock radio and turned back the covers on the queen-size bed. The ten minutes seemed like an hour.

Katie finally emerged. She stood just outside the bathroom door, eyes afire, looking exultant. Her full-bodied blonde hair fell in waves over her shoulders. Bulging over the top of the bustier, her breasts were poised, nipples erect. Garters held her black stockings, which had snowflake-patterned highlights. JB was briefly stunned by her alluring beauty, and then he approached her.

"Merry Christmas!" she said, turning her hip toward him, showing off the holiday pattern of her stockings.

"Oh, Katie!" he said as he drew her in his embrace. "You look good enough to eat!"

"Oh, so it *is* dessert," she said, laughing, and she sat on the bed. JB held up her left leg, gently fondling it, sliding his hand over the sheer fabric toward her groin. "Ummm," she responded. Her pubic area was smooth-shaven, except for a thin line of blonde hairs in the center, her "Mohawk", she called it. JB kneeled between her legs, eager to taste his after-dinner treat. It seemed odd, he was thinking, that he had never enjoyed holiday shopping before.

At the Mecklenburg sheriff's office, Detective Bruce Duffer was seeking a morning cup of bean. He found the dog warden, Tom Carlson, in the break room, pouring himself a cup of coffee.

"Hey, Tom," greeted Duffer, reaching for his own mug.

"G' morning, Bruce." Tom was wearing a brown county officer's coat.

"Are you heading out this morning?"

"Yeah. A dead deer in the road."

"Seems like a lot this year."

"Maybe. It's out near Beechwood Point again. Must be a herd of them out there or something."

"I guess," said Duffer.

"Have you heard any more on the sheriff's election?"

"As a matter of fact, yes. Ronnie Malcom has been collecting signatures to be put on the ballot."

"Ronnie Malcom? Isn't he a state trooper?" asked Tom.

"Yeah. I've worked several cases with him. He's up for retirement next year. He's a damned good law enforcement officer."

"Would you vote for him?"

Bruce glanced out the door into the hall before answering in a lowered voice. "Probably. I'm not sure Skylar has enough experience yet."

"Yeah. I know what you mean!" He took a gulp of coffee and

patted Bruce on the shoulder. "Well, I'm off in my deer hearse! See you later."

Bruce carried his coffee back to his office, and Betsy handed him his mail as he walked by. He found the envelope from the ME's office with the final results of the double-suicide case. Rachel Avery had been deemed a suicide. A single contact wound by a rifle bullet had been discovered in the dried blood under her chin. The right-side head wound that had bled down to the jaw had actually been the exit wound. Her blood alcohol had been 0.162, twice the 0.080 legal threshold for intoxication. Her boyfriend, however, had been a bit more intoxicated, with his blood alcohol measuring 0.235. His death had also been a suicide. The extra shot markings in the ceiling remained a mystery, possibly a test shot or a botched first attempt from a last-second change of mind. Nonetheless, the case was closed.

Chapter 11

During the two weeks before Christmas, the Boydton Baptist Church had several weeknight events to accommodate their children's nativity play and the choir's cantata. The Sunday-before-Christmas service, for additional celebration, featured Bruce Duffer singing with his acoustic guitar. Outside of the church, few knew of the detective's latent talent. He sang the Alabama Christmas song "Joseph and Mary's Boy."

"The gift is just what's in your heart, and not what's in your hand ..."

His instrumentation and harmony were rich and splendorous, eliciting applause from the congregation, a rarity during a worship service. To Duffer, music was an escape from the intensity of homicide investigation. Additionally, that Sunday's performance allowed him to sing praises to Jesus for his birthday.

After church, the worshippers milled about in front of the church. Duffer received repeated praise about his solo. A medium-built, mustached man approached and spoke to him. "Mr. Duffer, I thoroughly enjoyed hearing you sing."

"Thanks."

"I came today because I heard that you would be singing. Do you play any outside of the church?"

"Not really. Just around the house."

"Well, I'm Gil Carmichael. We're forming a little bluegrass band, a foursome, and we're looking for an acoustic guitar accompanist."

"Oh really?"

"Yeah. From what I've seen, you'd be good at it."

"Oh, well, I hadn't thought of doing anything like that before." But Duffer found the idea intriguing.

"Okay, but think about it. We usually practice on Thursday nights. It's pretty fun! We've only learned about four songs, but we've been asked to play at the Horseshoe Café."

"All right. I may be interested. I'll have to look over my work schedule and see if it's do-able."

"Great! Thanks Mr. Duffer," said Gil. "Here's my number." He handed Duffer a card.

"It's Bruce. And thank *you!*"

He discussed the band invitation with his wife, Joanne, who knew how much playing music de-stressed him. It was an alternative to alcohol for her nondrinking man. She encouraged his participation. The Thursday after Christmas, Bruce found himself in Gil Carmichael's basement. He joined the banjo player, bass fiddler, lead guitarist, and a fourteen-year-old dynamo of the strings, Joshua Carmichael, on mandolin. Their peppy rhythm projected such a joyous sound that even those who might not be bluegrass fans would be captivated. He felt at home with this band.

"So, what's this band called?" asked Bruce.

"Buggs Island Bluegrass," answered Gil.

The South Hill Rescue crew entered the ER with a patient for evaluation. Dr. Hardy reviewed the patient's profile in the electronic record and discovered he'd had four recent ER visits. This seemed like excessive emergent care for a twenty-three-year-old. His diagnoses predominantly involved fainting or seizure spells, sometimes tainted by drug usage. There was a question of malingering raised as well. Dr. Hardy looked up at the exam area to find a slender black male, alert, smiling, and not obviously ill.

A stout EMT, holding his Toughbook electronic ambulance call log, approached Dr. Hardy.

"The call went out as *seizures*," he said. "We've picked him up before, and his history is a little confusing."

"Yeah. I've reviewed his record," said Hardy.

"Well, Doc, it's a little embarrassing, but I think I've made the diagnosis," said the EMT with a sheepish grin. "He was shaking about in the ambulance, not like a typical seizure. I decided to just give him some Versed anyway. So, I bent over to get it out of the med box, and when I did, I passed some gas."

"You farted?"

"Yeah. Out loud," said the EMT, nodding. "And he sprung right up and started laughing!"

Dr. Hardy burst out in laughter. "Well, I'm sure that's *not* in the textbooks as a test for pseudoseizures!" He knew that it would be very difficult to standardize the dosing of first responders' "laughing gas."

Chapter 12

The term car wash often conjures images of a high-school fundraiser with bikini-clad cheerleaders and bubbles. In cold weather, it's not a prominent thought among drivers. Winter road-maintenance regimens, however, leave automobiles stained with gritty sand and salt. These harsh elements can dull body paint and catalyze corrosion of metal. This is what led to JB's continued business despite the low temperatures. JB's "specials" also spanned all seasons.

A blue Camaro drove out from JB's car wash onto the roadway. It travelled about a block before turning left onto another town street. A *whoop-whoop* sound erupted as a county police car appeared behind the vehicle, blue lights flashing. Officer Ted Johnson approached the driver's door. He was stout and medium height at best. His appearance resembled that of a marine drill sergeant. Puffs of vapor appeared in the cool air as he spoke. "License and registration, please."

"Sure, officer," said the driver. He handed him the requested items. "What seems to be the problem?"

"Unsignalled turn," he answered flatly.

"Oh? I'm sorry. It was just that there were no other vehicles on the road. I didn't think about signaling."

"I was on the road. Parked over there." He pointed toward the car wash. Handing the driver the ticket, he gave a wicked smile. "Be careful from now on. Have a nice day."

As officer Johnson retreated to his vehicle, the driver rolled up his window. "Damn! What an asshole!"

The county cruiser returned to its position across the road from the car wash. It wasn't the driver that had been targeted by law enforcement. It wasn't even the sports car. It was the establishment patronized that had provoked the traffic stop.

JB had taken notice of the deputy's actions and knew it would be bad for his business. Several county police officers were repeat customers of his. He wondered what might be the motivation behind this harassment.

"You know who that is, don't you?" said Al, his car wash coworker.

"No. Do you?" asked JB.

"Yeah. Deputy Johnson." JB looked at Al, then turned his gaze to the police car.

Katie Johnson, thought JB. "Oh, I see."

JB poured a cup of coffee from the pot in the car wash office and walked across the street to the stakeout site. It was time to meet the parents. He smiled pleasantly and tapped on the car window.

"Officer, it's chilly out here, and I thought you might appreciate a cup of coffee." He held out his steaming gift.

Lowering his window, Officer Johnson peered grimly at JB. He took the cup and glanced at it.

"It's *black!* I should've figured as much!" He threw the hot beverage at JB, who jumped back quickly.

"Ow! That's hot!"

"Yeah. They call us the heat. And you're gonna feel it!" The window glass rose up and closed completely.

JB retreated to the car wash and texted Katie. "Just had coffee with your dad."

"Oh? How did it go?"

"Not enough CREAM for his taste!"

"Oh. Sorry. ☹"

The next two days found no relief from the police pressure on JB's clients. Charged offenses included unfastened seat belts, expired state inspections, and failure to completely stop at stop signs. When a bronze-colored pickup drove into the car wash, JB went out to meet the driver before he could get out. Wayne Dodson had a box of Glistex sitting on the passenger side.

"Sorry, man," said JB, looking over to where the county cruiser was stationed. "I'm being hassled by the po-po. My *specials* business is shot right now!"

"Humph," responded Wayne. He glared at the deputy in obvious disdain.

"I'll contact you when I'm up and running again. Be careful."

"Awright," he grumbled. As he pulled out from the car wash, he gave Deputy Johnson a threatening gaze. It seemed effective, as his departure did not elicit police pursuit.

Detective Duffer sat amongst a crop of paperwork at his work desk. Several of his recent cases had gone cold, with no sparks of evidence or new leads. Betsy had printed out the new CODIS inquiry results. Understandably, the first run on the Garner case handkerchief had found no matches. Since the murderer was now likely dead himself, Duffer had asked for a speculative relative run. This would look for possible first- and second-generation relatives who shared ninety percent or more haplotypes with the suspect. This had yielded matches, but, unfortunately, there were 257 of them. Now came the arduous task of throwing out the chaff and identifying a suspect family. Even in the modern age of scattered relatives, there were clusters of apples that had fallen close to the family tree. Hence, there were high densities of hits in Virginia and North Carolina but apparently random distributions of others in a dozen states. Duffer needed to narrow the field.

He beckoned to Betsy.

"Yes, Bruce?"

"Can you check these matches for current status? You know, like dead, alive, incarcerated?"

"I guess so. How soon do you need it?"

"No great rush." After all, it had been sixty-five years. Another week would make little difference.

Chapter 13

The January sky was a gray blanket, with a single blur of sunlight glowing as through a threadbare area of the fabric. Below the Kerr Dam, the parking area seemed unwelcoming on a winter afternoon. Detectives Bruce Duffer and Carl Wilborne parked the county cruiser across the lot from an unattended, faded-orange pickup truck with a camper shell over the bed. They were investigating a missing person.

Ralph Forman, the pickup's owner, had last been seen three days before, when he'd come to the area to fish for stripers. When he hadn't returned home, his family had reported him missing. Detective Wilborne looked out over the steep bank of large granite rocks down to the water.

"You think he drowned, Bruce?" he queried.

Bruce peered out along the jagged stone shoreline. "Possibly. But where's his rod and tackle? Do you think they fell in as well?"

"Or maybe someone else found them and took them."

"Yeah. Maybe." He handed Wilborne a pair of blue rubber gloves. "Let's do this."

They dusted the doors and nonporous interior surfaces. They found several decent prints and lifted them to run for matches if circumstances required. Duffer made an observation as they were finishing. "It's odd. He was here to fish, but there are no rods or tackle here."

"That's right," said Wilborne.

"And the family said he always kept a 12-gauge shotgun in his truck."

"No guns here."

Duffer suspected this was not an accidental drowning or a routine missing person. He sensed something more sinister was likely.

"Something's just fishy," said Duffer. Wilborne chuckled at the grim humor.

A truck with a rollback winch arrived and hooked up the pickup. When the rollback headed off to the impound, Duffer and Wilborne drove off as well. As they approached the Beechwood Point area, they noticed the county animal control truck parked on the shoulder. Tom Carlson was dragging an animal carcass. Curiosity led them to stop and offer assistance.

"Can we give you a hand?" asked Duffer.

"Yeah. Thanks," said Tom. "Grab an end."

Duffer donned another pair of blue gloves and grabbed the deer's hind legs. They lifted the doe up, and it thumped into the truck bed.

"That's the fifth deer killed along here this year," said Tom.

"So, do you think there's a deer trail crossing the road around here?" asked Duffer.

"Maybe so. Deer on the highway can be very unpredictable, but several drivers have reported some bizarre behaviors."

"Like what?" asked Wilborne.

"Well, some said that the deer appeared to stagger and sway. Others reported that their heads bobbed about."

"Like they were drunk?" said Wilborne.

"I guess so. I'm gonna send this carcass to the Virginia Tech research lab. I want them to check it for toxins or diseases."

"You'd expect road kills from intoxicated drivers," said Duffer, "not from 'deer under the influence'—DUIs!"

Chapter 14

Dr. Hardy was working the daytime shift in the South Hill ER and was in the last hour of duty. He was questioning a seventeen-year-old male patient about his injury.

"So, just how did you get this animal bite?"

"Well, we were in the woods, coon hunting, and the dogs found this possum," said the boy.

"A possum?"

"Yeah." The adolescent looked a bit embarrassed. "He was in this old tire and was distracting the coon dogs. I was pulling him out with a stick, and the stick broke. He bit my thumb." He held out his thumb, which had only a small scratch on it.

"Did you kill the possum?" asked Dr. Hardy.

"Yeah. But we threw it in the woods."

No carcass for rabies testing, thought Dr. Hardy.

An opossum was not an aggressive mammal, so its bites were uncommon. Since Dr. Hardy had never treated one before, he checked the online site of the Center for Disease Control for risk assessment. He confirmed the rarity of rabies in the species but took the precautious route of ordering a rabies vaccination series. It was likely that this woodlands warrior would experience a more risky animal bite in future and would benefit from this protection.

"Dr. Hardy," said the ER unit secretary. "There's a Detective Duffer out front who wants to speak with you."

"Okay. Well, I can meet with him in the quiet room," said Dr. Hardy. That room was used for meeting with the families of critically ill or dying patients. It was presently vacant. He headed to the room, where he saw the detective.

"What's up, Bruce?" asked the doctor.

"Oh, just some ME stuff I wanted to run by you," said Duffer. "Did you hear about Ralph Forman, the fisherman missing from the dam three weeks ago?"

"Yeah, I did. Did he end up dead or something?"

"Well, yes, but not in Virginia. His body was found in Manson, North Carolina, five days later. He was murdered."

"I was afraid of that. So I guess, since it was in North Carolina, then it's out of your jurisdiction. And it isn't your case anymore. Right?"

"Well, not technically. His body was located in a wooded area within six miles of the dam. We're working with the Warren County police, and I requested the autopsy report from Raleigh. Some of the findings were disturbing and caught my attention." He handed the doctor a manila folder. "I was hoping you would review the report and clarify some details for me."

"Sure." Dr. Hardy studied the three-page postmortem summary. It showed the basic measurements: height, 69 inches, weight, 172 pounds, and general description. The man had been wearing a T-shirt, flannel shirt, underwear, and jeans. The gross examination had reported the torso as having multiple stab wounds. "The last one we had with stabbings was that one from the lake."

"Yes. Vance Kort," said the detective. "And he was found just downstream from where this one's abandoned truck was parked."

"Oh yeah?"

"And check out page 2," added Duffer.

Dr. Hardy studied the next page. Part of the scalp had been excised. "Oh no! Another scalping?" he exclaimed. "Like the one from the grave?"

"Yep. Victor Soloman. I'm thinking that we may have a serial killer."

66

"But Kort wasn't scalped, was he?"

"No. But remember, he was also bald. He had no hair for a trophy."

"Yeah, you're right." The doctor continued studying the report. "So there's evidence here of sexual assault as well?"

"Yes. They concluded he had sodomy performed on him."

"'Small anal abrasions without bleeding, consistent with postmortem injuries,'" read Dr. Hardy. "There was no semen found, so we can assume a condom was used."

"Yep. No DNA," said Duffer. "But take a look at the skin on the lower back."

"'Evidence of blood smears and hair follicles,'" Hardy read aloud. "Hmm ... do you think the murderer put the man's scalp on his low back while he sexually assaulted his body?"

"It appeared that way to me."

"That's even sicker!"

"Well, I thought maybe with the scalp pelt placed on the buttocks, the hair made it look more like a female that he was screwing," speculated the detective.

"I guess it would. I've never heard of such a crime."

"So, we could be looking for a perverted, homosexual serial killer."

"One who likes knives," added Dr. Hardy. He felt a chill spread over his body.

"Definitely!" Then, in a somber tone, Duffer added, "It's imperative that we keep this confidential."

"Oh, certainly." If the public knew there might be a serial killer running loose in Mecklenburg County, panic would greatly hamper the investigation.

Chapter 15

It was a Tuesday morning when Detective Bruce Duffer answered a call to JB's Car Wash. Al had phoned the sheriff's office when JB had not come in to work for the second day. At the car wash, Duffer began gathering more information from JB's coworker.

"So, when did you last see JB?" asked the detective.

"It was on Saturday. We closed up around two o'clock. He didn't show up yesterday, and I didn't think much of it. We'd been a little slow, and I could handle things okay by myself."

"Did he call you or anything?"

"Well, he did send me a text. Something about his girlfriend."

"Do you still have that text?"

"Yeah. I guess so." Al fingered his cell phone and showed the result to the detective: "Woman trouble today. Will see you later."

"Hmm," said Duffer. "Do you know anything about this relationship? He's not married, right?"

"Oh no. He's single. But he's been seeing that deputy's daughter, though. Deputy Johnson."

"Ted Johnson?"

"Yeah," said Al, nodding. "He keeps a close watch over JB too! He sits in his squad car across the street here a lot."

"Do you happen to know where Deputy Johnson's daughter works? She might know where he is." His first thought was that they might have sneaked off, out from under her father's strict scrutiny.

"She works at a bank in Chase City, I think."

"Okay. I can find her. I may go by JB's residence on Skipwith Road as well," said Duffer.

"Okay. But his car wasn't home last night. I checked that out myself."

"Thanks. I'll keep you updated." He didn't reveal to Al that his last missing-person case hadn't ended well. Maybe this was just a brief clandestine romantic escape.

Duffer learned that Katie Johnson worked at Farmers Bank, so he drove to Chase City to talk with her. She was at work that day, and he met with her in the office break room. Katie was neatly dressed in a business-style skirt and blouse. She appeared quite anxious that the detective had come to speak with her.

"Katie Johnson," he said, "I'm Detective Bruce Duffer."

"Yes, I know," said Katie. She was wringing her hands nervously.

"Do you know Jerome Benjamin? They call him JB."

"Yes." She nodded, her voice quivering. "Is … is he okay?"

"Well, we don't know yet. He's been reported missing."

"Oh my God!" Katie covered her mouth, and her eyes filled with tears. The detective paused a moment before continuing.

"When did you last see him, Katie?" Duffer was calm and empathetic.

"Uh … Sunday afternoon. We … we had a fight." She lowered her head, and her body trembled. "I told him we needed to break up. My dad's been harassing us, forbidding me to see him. I threatened to move out. I couldn't take the pressure!"

"I'm sorry, Katie. Do you know where he might have gone?"

"No. Not really." She looked up at Duffer, tears creeping down her cheeks. "I'm afraid he may have done something."

"What do you mean?"

"We texted Sunday night. He said he couldn't *live* without me."

"Did you keep the texts?"

"Yeah." She picked up her cell phone and manipulated the screen. Detective Duffer read the messages.

"If we can't be together, I can't go on." She scrolled to his final message. "Good bye. Remember, I love you."

"Have you spoken to him since then?" asked the detective.

"No. He won't answer or return my texts. I've been worried sick! I didn't know what to do!" Desperation showed in her face.

"Katie, do you know any place he might go if he wanted to get away from things or relax?"

"Well, he liked the Castle bar." She paused but then spoke suddenly. "Oh, he used to go fishing to relax."

"Okay. Do you know anywhere that he liked to fish at?"

"Uh … a pond! Yeah! Out near Beechwood Point. There's an abandoned farmhouse there. He used to hang out there a lot as a teenager."

"Yeah. I think I know where that is. I'll go check it out. If you remember anything else, you can call and let me know."

"Okay. Sure." She nodded.

Detective Duffer drove directly to the deserted house at Beechwood Point, the old Garner home. The spring sky spread vividly overhead, with occasional cotton-like clouds drifting lazily by. He imagined it would make a great hangout for a teenager—a house, a yard, a pond, and no adults. He walked up to the building and noted that the grass was flattened in a parallel line pattern, as if by vehicle tires. The ground was not damp enough for tire-tread tracks. He looked down over the pond. It was probably two acres in size, but the banks were not steep, which usually indicated shallow water. A vehicle in the pond would be incompletely submerged and obviously visible.

The following morning he returned with an investigative team. Skylar Daniels took charge of the on-site scene search. Carl Wilborne and Ted Johnson began walking the pond perimeter, looking for vehicle tracks or other suspicious findings. Bruce Duffer took photos of the marks in the grass. He noticed something metallic alongside one of the marks on the grass. It was a silver-colored man's wristwatch. He photographed it from several angles and then collected the item in a plastic bag.

Ted Johnson appeared distracted, not focusing on his assignment. After fifteen minutes of cursory searching, he approached Skylar Daniels near the house.

"So, Skylar, what's your take on this?" he asked.

"I don't know. I'm not seeing any signs of a crime scene here."

"Well, we don't know there's been any crime. Just a missing nigger," said Johnson.

"Well, it appears he was depressed and desperate. We're worried about a suicide."

Johnson spread out his arms. "Where? Do you see anything? We're wasting time and efforts!" Then, taking a serious tone, he continued. "What if he did do something? He'll turn up sooner or later. We can invest our law-enforcement resources then."

"Maybe so."

"You know, this is the election year. Careful budgeting could be an asset for you. I can spread the word, if you know what I mean."

"All right," agreed Skylar after a pensive pause. He called out to the others, "Carl, Bruce! Let's wrap it up. I don't see anything exciting here."

Deputy Johnson smiled in satisfaction.

Chapter 16

It was a day off for Dr. Hardy as he and his wife prepared to go out to dinner. They were going to one of their favorite restaurants, Cooper's Landing, in nearby Clarksville. Hardy had chosen a short-sleeved dress shirt and was considering accessories.

"Do you think I need a tie?" he asked Lucy.

"Naw. I'm just wearing a skirt," she said, continuing to curl her hair. Dr. Hardy's cell phone suddenly buzzed with a call. He placed it on speaker phone while he put on his socks.

"Hello. It's Dr. Hardy here."

A female voice replied. "Hi. This is Investigator Phillips at the medical examiner's office. Are you available for a scene visit?"

"Yeah, I guess so." Hardy looked at his wife. "Where is it?"

"Clarksville."

"Okay." Dr. Hardy got the address and info. He turned to Lucy. "How about a dinner cruise, dear?"

"What?"

"There's an ME case on the lake in Clarksville. I need to go there before we eat dinner."

"Well, I'd rather have had a margarita as an appetizer, but I'll go with you."

Dr. Hardy drove them in the Jeep, uncertain as to what terrain they might encounter. It was in a sparsely populated residential area outside of the town, where there were three lakefront homes in a wooded cul-de-sac. One of the disadvantages of being a local medical examiner was the blemished view one acquired of the community. Few things made more of an impression than the site of a dead body, often revealing violent circumstances. Each location of a death scene became permanently burned vividly into memory, as a morbid tattoo on the brain. Travelling past these sites triggered vibrant visions of fatalities, forever tainting one's perspective of the area. If asked, Dr. Hardy could speckle a county map with black pins, marking the hundreds of ME calls he had worked.

This scene was marked by a county cruiser and a tan-colored van labeled Mecklenburg County Dive Team. Dr. Hardy carried his navy-colored nylon ME bag and Lucy a clipboard and pen.

Detective Duffer met them at the Jeep. Abandoning the search of the old Garner place earlier had freed him up for this case. "Hi, Doc. The residents here discovered this body about three." He began walking down toward the dock behind the house. "They've offered to carry us out to the location."

The doctor and Lucy followed Duffer to the shore and onto the wooden dock. The lake water was a reddish-brown color, muddy from recent rain runoff. There seemed to be a lot of leaves and sticks floating about the cove. A middle-aged man wearing a life jacket sat at the wheel of a pontoon boat.

"Hello. Grab yourself a life jacket," said the man.

Lucy stepped onto the deck in her platform sandals and skirt. Dr. Hardy handed her an orange life preserver. He realized they were a bit overdressed for this cruise.

"Mr. Robbins noted an odor this morning and thought it was from a dead fish or the trash washing up in the cove. When it worsened, he came out to investigate," said Duffer.

The outboard motor started, and they made their way along the edge of the debris "slick" composed of driftwood, leaves, and paper and plastic garbage. The flotsam stretched out over fifty yards from the downstream bank at the mouth of the cove. The boat slowed as they approached the dive team's boat. A tan object barely breaking the surface bobbed in the water beside two divers.

"We've got the underwater pictures already," announced Detective Wilborne from the divers' boat. "Let me know when you're ready to move it, Doc."

"Okay," said Dr. Hardy. He was, however, only able to see a bare back, a head, and trousers along the waist area. "Lucy, can you take a few photos of the body and the floating debris?"

"Yeah, sure." She aimed her smartphone and took some shots.

"It's okay to move the body now," said Hardy.

Dragging a body onto a private citizen's boat was not an option. The dive boat was a V-hull with high sides. To wrestle a wet corpse up over the side would be quite a chore.

"We have a mesh body bag we can use," said Detective Wilborne.

"Yeah!" said Duffer. "We could drag it alongside the boat to the beach."

As the divers packaged the body, Duffer, Hardy, and Lucy transferred onto the dive boat. The divers climbed aboard, and the group began to slowly troll along the lake. Moving through the water while dragging a body could easily dislodge particles of evidence, so their progress was impeded. It took twenty minutes to round the point and reach the beach a half mile away. This site was where the road access was closest to the shore.

Duffer took the lead once making land and, with the divers standing in the shallows, lifted the body onto the sandy beach. It lay facedown on the nylon netting.

"Okay, Doc," said Duffer.

Dr. Hardy began examining the body. It was a black person, wearing only sweatpants, whose skin was grayed by prolonged immersion in the water. The hair was black, curly, and about two or three inches long in a non-gender-specific style. The crotch of the pants was torn open, and the doctor peered through the hole to identify the sex of the corpse. Decay had destroyed the tissues to the degree that no genitals or anus remained.

Another sexless corpse! he thought. He had worked only one other case in which the body had had no genitals. That one was a dead baby that had been tossed into an outdoor toilet. "There are no genitals," he said.

"Oh, but she's definitely a female!" said one of the divers. He then reached down and rolled the body onto its back. The breast mounds, shaped like cones, stood firmly erect, with exaggerated, water-engorged nipples. The eyelids and lips were tightly swollen, making facial recognition impossible.

"This one's definitely for the Richmond office," said Dr. Hardy. "She'll need the works!"

"I'll agree with that," said Duffer. "I'm not aware of any missing females reported in Mecklenburg County."

"I'll fax them what we've got so far."

"All right. Thanks, Doc."

After completing the scene visit, the Hardys continued to the restaurant. A vigorous handwashing ensued before they settled at a table. They each began with a glass of wine to help them relax. For Dr. Hardy, the memory of their awful death-scene visit began to dissipate.

"So, what are you hungry for?" he asked Lucy.

"I'm not sure." She leaned in toward him. "To tell you the truth, I've lost my appetite a bit."

"Yeah. Me too. At least for oysters on the half shell!"

The waitress approached their table with a friendly smile. "Can I tell you about our specials today?"

"Sure," said Dr. Hardy.

"We have broiled catfish or stuffed flounder."

Lucy met Hardy's gaze. "I'll just have a salad," she said.

Chapter 17

At his office, Detective Duffer carried some papers to Betsy's desk. He had organized the details of the stabbing and scalping deaths: Victor Soloman (shallow-grave scalping), Vance Kort (stabbed body from lake), and Ralph Forman (North Carolina case).

"Betsy, can you post these in the National Crime Information Center for me?" He was familiar with the NCIC listings, although he had seldom used the system.

"The FBI database?" she asked.

"Yeah. I'm looking for any related crimes or MOs."

"Sure. I can do it today."

"Thanks."

Duffer left the office, driving to JB's car wash, where he found Al still running the business. The detective showed him the watch he had found at the Garner homestead, in its plastic evidence bag.

"Al, is this JB's watch?" he asked.

Al took the bag and studied it briefly. "I think so. He had a watch like this."

"Can you be certain?" asked Duffer.

"Not absolutely," said Al, handing the item back to Duffer. "It sure looks like it, though."

"Well, thanks. You've been helpful."

The detective's next meeting was with Katie at the bank. It proved to be more fruitful.

"Oh yeah! That's his watch!" Katie said immediately.

"Are you sure about that?" Duffer asked.

"Absolutely! Girls have an eye for jewelry. We don't miss a detail. It's JB's watch. Where did you get it?"

"I found it near the fishing pond you told me about."

"Do you think he drowned?" She was visibly shaken.

"I don't know, yet. It's just a clue in his disappearance. We're still actively investigating his case."

Katie appeared to be digesting the information, briefly, before she began to cry softly.

Detective Duffer touched her shoulder reassuringly. "I'll let you know whenever we find out anything."

Katie just nodded.

The Occoneechee State Park outside of Clarksville was host to an annual music festival. Although jazz music was the theme, Buggs Island Bluegrass had been awarded a spot this spring. Bruce Duffer unpacked his guitar and tuned up with Gil Carmichael and the boys. They were gathered behind the stage area of the amphitheater, awaiting their time slot. This was a welcomed reprise from the stress of his investigative work. Bruce gazed across the lake to help relax before their performance. The blue, rippled waters gave no hint of the death and debris he had found just a week before only a mile upstream. When he turned back to their stakeout, he got a glimpse of the crowd. Instinctively, he scanned the group for suspicious persons. He did spot one: Skylar Daniels, in his police uniform. He was smiling and shaking people's hands. This was, needless to say, an election year, and it was less than six months until November. Skylar's politician's smile was uncharacteristically painted onto his face. Duffer shook his head. Hopefully, the voters would see through Skylar and realize that trooper Ronnie Malcom had the experience necessary to make a strong sheriff. For now, however, it was showtime. He picked up his guitar and hung the strap across his shoulder as the announcer called out, "Our very own Buggs Island Bluegrass!"

Dr. Hardy received his copy of the preliminary autopsy findings on the lake corpse with no gonads. It was indeed a female, aged twenty-five to thirty years. Her ID was still pending. The conclusion was that she most likely drowned, given the lack of signs of physical trauma and the circumstances surrounding her death. Toxicologies were still pending.

"It looks like that floater was a young adult, black female," he said to Lucy.

"I wonder what happened to her," she said.

"I don't know. Apparently, she had been dead for four to five days."

Dr. Hardy felt only an inkling of relief in the fact that she had not been stabbed or scalped. At least this death had not been at the hand of a twisted, sociopathic killer.

Dr. Hardy received a call from Detective Duffer the following day. The preliminary autopsy results had enabled him to identify the body. "She matched with a missing person from Danville," he said.

"Danville?" said Hardy. "That's fifty miles upstream!"

"Yeah. She was last seen five days before, walking along the rocky bank of the Dan River."

"That's at least ten miles a day of drifting. She was hauling ass!"

"Yep. One half to one mile per hour."

"I guess that's not so fast for the Dan River, but the backwaters of Buggs Island Lake are quite sluggish," said Hardy.

"I'm sure the recent rain runoff increased the flow rate."

"Well, at least she wasn't scalped!"

"Yeah. But she was also female, black, and three counties away."

"Oh, that's right." This case didn't fit the pattern of Mecklenburg County's lakeside murders.

Chapter 18

This time Dr. Hardy was on daytime ER duty when he received a call from the OCME's office.

"Are you available for a scene visit?" the investigator asked.

It was five fifty-two; a little more than an hour remained of his shift.

"Um, probably," said Hardy. He would need to get his colleague to cover the end of his shift. "Where is it?"

"It's called Beechwood Point. It's near Boydton."

"Okay. It'll probably take me thirty minutes or more."

"I'll let them know."

Dr. Hardy got the specifics and then turned off his phone. He turned to his coworker. "Alex, there's an ME case I need to work. Do you think I could leave a little early?"

His associate checked his computer screen for an overview. "Yeah, I guess. There's only two in the waiting room. We look pretty good here for now," said Alex.

"Okay. I'm admitting the heart failure in room 9, and I'll print out discharge instructions for room 3. She's a pyelonephritis, getting her IV antibiotic. Her temp has come down, and she can go after the med's in."

"All right. Tony's coming in at seven. He's never late."

"Great! Thanks!"

It was still 6:40 by the time Dr. Hardy reached Beechwood Point. A county police cruiser was parked at the driveway entrance, making the site easy to locate. An officer near the vehicle approached Dr. Hardy's Jeep. Hardy recognized Skylar Daniels, the sheriff's assistant.

"Dr. Hardy, they're up there near the house," he told him.

"Okay, thanks!" said Hardy.

It was warm and humid, a typical late-June day for southern Virginia. The windless air and cloudy sky seemed ideal for gnats and mosquitoes. As Hardy reached the house area, he was met by Detective Duffer. Duffer appeared sweaty, with his white shirt wet in the areas of his chest and armpits.

"Hardy, some people fishing in a canoe found this one. It's a black male in an SUV."

"A car? In that pond?"

"Yep."

The pond was just modest in size and didn't appear deep enough to hide a vehicle. The tow-truck winch activated with a loud whine. Hardy watched as the red automobile slowly rose from the pond. The rear end was first to emerge from the muddy water.

"The divers have taken pictures already," said Duffer over the drone of the winch. "The body's in a body bag, and they're bringing it ashore. He was floating facedown in the vehicle with his legs out of the driver's window. His knees were flexed so that his feet floated above the roof. The soles of his shoes were what the fishermen noticed."

"So, he wasn't belted in?"

"No."

"If it was a suicide, wouldn't he have buckled himself in to assure he would drown?" asked Hardy.

"Yeah, maybe. He might have wanted his head to hit something so he might drown while unconscious. We're not sure if the window was rolled down or busted out, either."

"Do you have an ID yet?"

"Well, the body's not recognizable, but it's presumed to be Jerome Benjamin Tyler."

"JB? The car wash man?"

"Yeah. He's been missing for three weeks."

"Damn! That's such a waste!"

Hardy sensed some frustration from Duffer. "Well, we searched out here earlier and didn't find any tire track marks along the pond's edge. I think the vehicle went airborne, traveling off this embankment, and crashed into the water."

"So, not likely accidental, huh?"

"Nope." The detective had a serious tone. He turned away from the wrecked auto. "I think the body's down here."

Dr. Hardy eased down the grassy embankment to where Detective Wilborne and the two divers were working to move a white vinyl mass from the water. The divers apparently didn't have another mesh bag like the one they had used in the lake. Maneuvering the body about in the pond water wasn't too arduous, given the advantage of buoyancy. But the plastic body bag, essential in preserving loose elements of evidence, had taken on gallons of water in the packaging process. The vinyl sack now weighed 350 to 400 pounds and had no handles to aid in lifting or dragging. The wet, slippery shore made for sloppy footing as Detective Wilborne and a crash-truck rescue worker tugged on the unyielding load.

"What if we unzip it some down there? We might could drain some water out," Wilborne suggested.

"Okay," agreed a diver. But after a few heaves, he added, "Wait! When you pull up, some water flows out. But when you stop, it sinks back down and fills up again."

"All right. We'll have to keep tension on the bag between pulls," said Wilborne. However, the more of the load that became beached, the more buoyancy was lost and the heavier it became.

As the wrestling match ensued, the daylight was fading. The frogs began their nocturnal croaking, and Dr. Hardy found himself slapping at the mosquitoes biting his arms. He retrieved the thermometer that he had placed in the pond water. It read 82.4 degrees. A wet, earthy, swamp-like odor hung in the humid air. It was the intensified smell of the retrieved SUV. The doctor gloved up and grabbed hold of the body bag to help with the battle. Finally the load was on solid ground, with water streaming from the unzipped lower end.

"All right, Doc. He's all yours!" said Wilborne.

Dr. Hardy unzipped the upper part of the wet bag. The body emitted a fetid smell, much like dead fish. It was a black male, fully clothed, his feet hidden in the murky fluid pooled in the lower end. A few tadpoles squirmed about on the decedent's shirt. Hardy palpated the head and moved the neck, finding no evidence of broken bones. He pulled up the T-shirt, revealing skin sloughing over the torso.

"No obvious fractures or penetrating injuries," announced Dr. Hardy. "He's ready to go on to Richmond now."

"Okay," said Duffer from the top of the embankment. "We've called the funeral home already."

It was three weeks earlier that Duffer had presented Skylar with the watch and the car wash harassment reports. Skylar had been reluctant to activate the investigation then. Just three hours ago, Sheriff Larrimore had burst into Duffer's office, his imposing presence largely generated by his height and western-style hat, and the power in his voice completing his aura.

"Bruce, we've got a body!" he'd said.

"Where is it?" Duffer had responded.

"The old Garner place. In the pond."

"Is it JB?"

"We think so."

Bolting up, Duffer followed Larrimore out the doorway. In the sheriff's shadow was Skylar, standing just outside the door. Duffer thought he looked a bit sheepish. He had, admittedly, called off the area search prematurely. Even after Duffer's findings, he had still declined to pursue the leads.

"Betsy," said the sheriff, "call Homes's Garage and ask if he's en route yet."

"Sure, Sheriff Larrimore," she answered.

"Carl Wilborne's on the scene and called for a tow truck," Larrimore explained to Duffer. "The dive team's on the way there, too."

"Great," said Duffer. "Looks like you've got everything covered."

Clay Larrimore was in his lame-duck final term as sheriff. Usually one could coast through those final months, cashing in any unused vacation hours. Not Larrimore. He had taken up the reigns and assumed charge of this case. Commanding actions like this had won Duffer's respect and admiration.

Now, standing on the muddy bank with Duffer, Detective Wilborne spoke. "I've called Freeman's Funeral Home."

Chapter 19

Detective Bruce was in his office when Tom Carlson raced in. For an animal control officer, he was unusually excited.

"Bruce!" he shouted. "I got the toxicologies back on that roadkill deer!"

He placed a sheet of paper on Bruce's desk. Bruce was familiar with toxicologies and knew that *tetrahydrocannabinol* was a metabolite of cannabis.

"Marijuana?" said Bruce. "In a deer?"

"Yep! You know what this means, right? The deer that have been getting hit by cars were stoned!"

"Uh-huh. So …"

"So, there has to be a marijuana field nearby!"

"Ah! This is crazy, Tom," said Duffer. "I'll need to get some officers to search that area." *It seems that Beechwood Point has become a hotbed of crime*, he thought.

"Detective Duffer," said Betsy. She was standing in the doorway.

"Yes."

"I don't mean to interrupt, but the NCIC search results came in online. I've printed it out for you."

"Great. Thanks, Betsy," said Duffer. "Oh, and can you find Detective Wilborne for me? We need to organize a marijuana field search."

"Sure."

"Thanks for this tip, Tom," said Duffer. "Animal control officers don't usually contribute to drug investigations."

"Yep. It's usually just strays, animal bites, and roadkill."

Once alone again, Detective Duffer began reading the crime search printout. Oddly enough, there were two unsolved homicides with MOs similar to his three cases. Stranger still, they were in Texas. Both of the victims were males who had been stabbed to death. One of them also had documented sexual assault and scalping. This report put a twist in the Mecklenburg cases, a dismal one at that.

Texas? he thought. *How could this relate to killings in rural Virginia?* The similarities were too close to be merely coincidental. He continued studying the report and discovered that the sodomy case had yielded a semen DNA sample, but no data-bank matches had been made. The Texas murders had taken place four and five years ago. Maybe something new had been logged by now.

"Betsy," he said into his desk phone's page mode.

"Yes?"

"Could you run a current DNA profile in CODIS on the specimen from this Texas murder? Maybe there's something new now."

"Okay, Detective."

He hadn't disclosed to Betsy that he suspected a serial killer in Mecklenburg County. Nonetheless, she had posted the crime profiles and had seen the matches. He was sure she knew by now. It was time to take this investigation to a higher level. He did have a close associate in the Virginia State Police: Ronnie Malcom. Ronnie might take particular interest in a Mecklenburg County case since this was a sheriff's election year.

Shortly after Duffer had left him a message, Ronnie Malcom returned his call. They made an arrangement and then met at the sheriff's office after regular business hours, to avoid curious ears. Officer Malcom was tall, with short-trimmed hair, the typical features of state policemen. Duffer presented him with the connections he had found in the county cases, including the North Carolina body.

"I think you're onto something here, Bruce," said Malcom.

"And today I got the results of a NCIC search." He handed the printout to Ronnie. "I got this hit."

Ronnie Malcom studied the papers and looked up at Duffer. "Jesus Christ, Bruce!" he exclaimed. He was obviously shaken. "If this is the same perp, he is a real bad-ass dude! We have to find this demented pervert and put him away!"

"Amen!"

"I'm taking this to the FBI. We need their help with this one."

Detective Duffer was grateful for the recruited assistance, but he felt it was only a ray of hope in this darkening cloud of doom. That night, he resorted to his guitar to slow his racing thoughts and defuse some of his stress. Despite this, his sleep was fitful, and he was unrefreshed when he arrived back at work the following morning. He politely grumbled as he passed Betsy's desk. After a short wait, she timidly entered his office, bearing a cup of coffee.

"Detective Duffer," she said softly.

"Huh? Yes, Betsy?" She extended the coffee to him. "Oh … thank you!"

"I ran that updated DNA. You might want to look at this." She handed him a sheet of paper.

Duffer took a swallow of the fresh, steaming beverage. He removed his glasses, rubbed his eyes as if adjusting the focus, and then began to study the printout. The DNA had a partial match, still greater than 99 percent correlation. This corresponded to the speculative relative category. The type of match meant that the relationship was a second cousin or closer. *Too much science for this early hour*, he thought.

"Do you see the relative match?" asked Betsy.

He refocused his attention on the page. It seemed incredible!

"The Garner case sample?"

"Yep!"

Chapter 20

On his ER computer monitor, Dr. Hardy selected the patient waiting in exam 6. Mr. Lydick was a fifty-three-year-old male whose complaint was entered as "abdominal pain." Hardy scanned his vital signs, noting a temperature of 98.3. This made diagnoses of diverticulitis and appendicitis less likely. He was old enough for gallbladder stones to be common and still youngish for an abdominal aortic aneurysm. Next, the blood pressure was 138/85, too low to expect an aortic wall dissection. Somewhat assured that a catastrophic condition was unlikely, the doctor approached the patient's bedside.

"Mr. Lydick, I'm Dr. Hardy," he said, donning his blue latex-free, gloves. "Tell me what's going on with your stomach."

The patient was a well-groomed, middle-aged white man. He appeared in decent health.

"Well," he said, "it's with my bowels."

"Your bowels? What's wrong with them? Are you having diarrhea?"

"Uh ... no."

"Any stomach pains or vomiting?"

"Uh ... no, not that."

"Have you had any fever or cough?"

"No. It's ... it's something in my rectum."

"Something? Like what?" Dr. Hardy imagined a steak bone or maybe a swallowed bottle cap.

"Like ... a fingernail polish bottle or something." He looked a little embarrassed. "Silly girl," he added, as if to justify the situation.

"Well, I'll need to check it out," said Hardy.

The doctor lubricated a gloved finger and entered the cavernous rectum. Sure enough, he palpated a hard plastic object. Despite snaking his finger about, he could not secure a hold on the bottle. It just rolled about in the poop chute like an asteroid drifting weightlessly in space. After a two minute struggle, he abandoned the mission.

"I need to call in a specialist," he said to the patient. After two physician calls, he was able to convince a general surgeon to take on the case. Dr. Drummond requested that the ER staff prepare the patient for general anesthesia to allow him to remove the foreign body.

Nurse Patty brought Mr. Lydick the consent form for his procedure. After anesthesia, he would need someone to escort him home.

"Would you like me to give your wife a call?" she asked.

"Oh no! No!" he snapped. Then, softly, he added, "No, thank you. That won't be necessary." He quickly scribbled his name on the form.

"Okay. Dr. Drummond will be here shortly. Just sit tight." Patty retreated and approached Dr. Hardy's work station. "He certainly didn't want his wife to know he was here," she said.

"Oh?" said Hardy. "Oh, I see!" He realized that the spouse apparently was not the "silly girl."

It had been nearly two hours after Mr. Lydick left for the OR when he returned to the ER. He was followed by a frustrated-appearing Dr. Drummond, who reported back to Dr. Hardy.

"I'm sending him out to the medical college," he said. "I worked over an hour trying to grab or snare that bottle. I just couldn't get it out!"

The ER unit secretary approached Dr. Drummond. "Mr. Lydick's wife is here in the waiting room," she said.

"Good. I'll go out and talk to her." As he turned away, Nurse Patty touched his arm and drew up beside him.

"Ah, Dr. Drummond," she said. "Let me share something with you." She spoke quietly as they walked off toward the waiting area.

The remainder of Dr. Hardy's ER shift was more mundane. It was nearly eleven that night when he arrived home. While eating the warmed-over supper plate that Lucy had prepared hours earlier, he shared the fingernail-polish bottle story with her.

"E-e-e-w!" she said. "That's just nasty!"

"Yeah. It made me think of that sodomy murder in North Carolina, though."

"Oh," said Lucy. "That reminds me. You got a ME report from the central office today." She handed him the mail from the kitchen island.

Hardy opened the envelope and read through the report. "It's the autopsy report on JB." As he studied the document, he began chuckling.

"What's so funny about an autopsy report?" asked Lucy.

"Well, they found a live fish in the pond water still in the body bag!" Hardy imagined the staff unzipping a body bag and seeing something wiggling around. "Maybe they got a taste of what it's like out here in the trenches!"

There was no discernable trauma found, and the conclusion listed the death as caused by "presumed drowning." The toxicologies showed only a small amount of marijuana and an estimated alcohol level of 0.075 percent, just below the legal intoxication level. The manner of death was undetermined. Certainly this was not a natural death. This meant that law enforcement would need to determine whether it was an accident, suicide, or homicide.

"Hmm. Drowning they say," announced Hardy.

"So, was it a suicide?" asked Lucy.

"We can't say." He looked solemnly at her. "What the police say will swing this one way or the other. It might still be a homicide."

Chapter 21

Detective Duffer accompanied Sheriff Clay Larrimore to the meeting of the Mecklenburg County drug task force. This force was a joint team of county, state, and DEA—Drug Enforcement Agency—members targeting area street-drug trafficking. Larrimore addressed this month's meeting, standing in the conference room in front of the other officers. Beside him was a white eraser board with a map of the county painted on it.

"Men, we have an unusual development in the county. This points to a potential local marijuana operation. I'd like Tom Carlson, the animal control officer, to give us the details."

"Thanks, Sheriff Larrimore," said Carlson. "This year, I found a dramatic increase in the number of vehicular deer strikes. They seemed, especially, to cluster around the area of Beechwood Point." He pointed to an area on the map and marked it with a red X. "Some drivers reported odd movements by these animals. So, on a whim, I sent off toxicologies on one of the roadkills. We found it had high levels of cannabis metabolites—marijuana!"

"You think the deer were stoned?" asked Ronnie Malcom.

"Well, from the descriptions of their erratic behavior and the increase in roadkills, yeah!"

Amid the chuckles from other officers, Ronnie said, "What the hell?"

"So … we suspect there is a marijuana field near this area. Studies of deer activity patterns have shown daily ranges of 250 acres up to 2,700 acres out west. In southside Virginia, they usually travel less than a mile a day."

"Of course, that's when they're sober, right?" quipped an officer. Some classroom laughter followed.

"Well, yes. Anyway, I've laid out a one-mile radius from the epicenter of road strikes, here." He drew a circle centered on the X on Beechwood Point. "I suspect a marijuana field is within this perimeter," said Carlson.

"Such a small area as this," said Ronnie, "would be ideal for a drone camera search. I can get a state police drone to fly over the area."

Sheriff Larrimore, who had been leaning against the table edge, returned to the front. "Thanks, Tom," he said. "Now, on a more serious note," he continued, "Ronnie Malcom has some data to share with us. Officer Malcom." He nodded to Ronnie.

"Thanks, Sheriff." Ronnie paused before addressing the assembly in a somber tone. "Detective Duffer has done some extraordinary investigative work on some local murder cases. Unfortunately, he's discovered enough similarities for us to suspect that these crimes are the works of a serial killer."

A hush verified that he had captured the full attention of his audience. Detective Duffer felt a warm sensation flow over his head. Maybe it was a bit of pride but it was also a sense of ominous apprehension. His suspicions were becoming reality.

"The connections include several common features. These are stabbing, scalping, and sodomy—anal sexual assaults. Not every case has the full trilogy but usually at least two of the three features. There are three of these homicides in the area, two in Mecklenburg County, and the third may have occurred in our county. The body was later found in Manson, North Carolina."

"So, he's working in two states?" stated an attending officer.

"Well, Duffer's research revealed two additional cases with similar MOs in Texas. These were three years ago. So, these killings may be spread over three states—that we know of. I've contacted the FBI, and they plan to have one of their agents here within the week."

"In any event," he continued, "we need to exercise increased vigilance, and please, *please*, do *not* let this get out into the community! This could incite panic in the community but also, even worse, alert the killer that we are onto him."

"Detective Duffer, can you give us some further details?" asked Malcom.

"Sure, Ronnie." He addressed the group. "Officer Malcom gave a good synopsis of the killer's MO, involving elements of stabbing, scalping, and sodomy. All of the victims have been male. The bald men were not scalped, probably because they would not have made good 'trophies.' Evidence of sexual assaults in some cases may have been lost due to time delays at discovery or environmental factors. Therefore, the MOs might really match more completely than we can prove."

"So," commented an officer, "we have a stabbing, scalping, and sodomizing murderer?"

"Yes. We do."

"Then he's the Triple-S Killer?"

"Yeah, I guess that's an appropriate title."

Following the triple-S killer briefing, Detective Duffer returned to his office. Picking through his mail, he found an envelope from the central ME's office. It was the report on Jerome Benjamin Tyler, JB. Based on the degree of decomposition, his time of death was estimated to have been twenty to twenty-five days earlier. This was consistent with the date of his disappearance, twenty-four days before he was found. Toxicologies had been run on the hair follicles, showing only small amounts of marijuana. The cause of death was undetermined, presumed to be drowning, based on the circumstances.

At least it's not a stabbing or scalping, thought Duffer. The manner of death appeared on the surface to be a suicide, but

Duffer wasn't sure of it. The friction between him and Katie's father, Ted Johnson, raised an element of uncertainty.

"Betsy," he spoke into his phone system. "See if you can reach Sheriff Larrimore for me."

"Okay. Sure," said Betsy.

Her compliance was prompt. "Sheriff Larrimore is on the line, sir."

"Thanks! Sheriff, I was reviewing Jerome Benjamin's autopsy. How should we proceed with the manner of death?"

"Well, Bruce, Skylar feels it was a lovesick suicide and the case should be closed," said Larrimore.

"Maybe. But I feel funny about Johnson's behavior, particularly since his daughter was involved with JB."

"Yeah. But we've got no evidence to support anything illegal."

"Conveniently damaged by his delaying the search," Bruce added.

"I know. But again, no real evidence. I trust your instincts, Bruce. I'll tell you what. If you run across anything more concrete, let me know right away. Until we have something more, this was a suicide."

"Okay. Thanks." *Closed cases aren't always solved cases*, he thought.

Chapter 22

The phone rang at the Hardys' home, and Lucy answered it. She looked toward her husband and spoke. "Yeah, he's here." She handed him the cordless phone. "Bruce Duffer for you."

"Hello," said Hardy. "What's up?"

"Doesn't one of your relatives fly radio-controlled planes?" asked Duffer.

"Yeah, Butch, my brother-in-law. He's in a flying club in Henderson. Why?"

"We've got a state police drone to use for a marijuana search, but the pilot was not available. Do you think he would help us out?"

"Probably so." He addressed Lucy. "Do you think Butch would fly a police drone for police?"

"Yeah. I'm sure he'd love to," she said.

Butch was in his midsixties and appeared hearty, despite his balding head. His dark complexion hinted at the component of Native American ancestry in his blood. By midday, Dr. Hardy had driven him out to Beechwood Point, where Detective Duffer had asked them to meet. The air was calm on the hot and humid late-August day. Duffer was accompanied by Ronnie Malcom, and the two were already parked in the driveway to the Garner home.

"Isn't this the old Garner place?" asked Dr. Hardy.

"It sure is," answered Duffer.

"Why do you suspect there's any marijuana around here?" asked Hardy.

Duffer smiled and said, "Well, we've had a number of roadkill deer along here that were found to be under the influence."

"Stoned deer?"

"Yep. The wildwood weed."

Malcom gently lifted the white drone with its four propellers out of Duffer's car. He carefully placed it on the ground.

"You think you can fly this thing?" he asked Butch. Duffer handed the control pack to him.

The familiar flight control sticks drew a smile from Butch. "Oh yeah. I've flown helicopters with these. A quadcopter with only a light wind is a piece of cake!" Butch made a preflight inspection of the drone.

"It's battery powered," said Malcom. "Fully charged, with a spare battery for backup."

"Good. That'll give us plenty of time." Butch pointed out the joysticks on the remote control. "The left one is altitude. The right controls the direction and speed of flight. It takes someone about five to ten flights to get a good feel for it. And the camera?"

"Oh yeah. We have two receivers. This small screen attaches to the controller, and a larger monitor is on this laptop. I can record all the images as we go."

"Okay. Where to?"

"I thought we might search southwest of here first," said Duffer. "It's the most remote area."

The drone started humming and then lifted off to begin the search. Dr. Hardy looked back and forth between the drone and the computer screen in front of Trooper Malcom. The pond passed slowly across the screen and was replaced by wooded terrain as the robotic plane progressed. On past the woods, an old tobacco barn became visible. A few wisps of grayish smoke were rising from the log-hewn building.

"Hey!" said Duffer. "I saw smoke out in that direction six months ago! I thought it was a campfire."

"Do you think they still use that tobacco barn?" asked Malcom.

"Most growers cure with propane now," said Duffer. "That's certainly strange."

"And looky here," said Butch. Just past the barn appeared a patch of leafy green growth. It looked to be cultivated, and it covered about four to five acres, with a wooded perimeter.

"That looks like marijuana!" exclaimed Malcom excitedly.

"I'll hover in lower for a closer look," said Butch. He carefully toggled the altitude-control stick down. The plants grew larger on the computer screen until their characteristic star-patterned leaf structure became obvious.

"Bingo!" said Malcom. "This is our pot field!"

"Hey," said Duffer. "Do you think the dealer is curing his weed in that old barn?"

"Probably so!" Malcom replied.

"Butch, see if you can see a road in."

"Okay. Roger that," said Butch.

He expanded the search by making a circle over the area with an increasingly wide radius. This tactic remained futile.

"Our battery is getting low. I'm heading back in now," he said.

With a fresh battery, the drone resumed its mission. The dense trees obscured much of the ground detail. Despite trying varying angled approaches and altitudes, they could discover no access road. Butch returned the drone to base. "Well, I'm sorry we didn't find a road," he said.

"Oh, that's all right," said Trooper Malcom. "We got what we came for. Thanks so much for your help!"

"I guess we'll monitor this area to find our pot farmer," said Duffer.

As Dr. Hardy and Butch drove home from Beechwood point,

Butch spoke. "So, Obie, if someone eats venison meat from a stoned deer, can he get high?"

"I don't know," said Hardy. "People cook soups and brownies with pot. I guess that cooking doesn't destroy the cannabis."

"I reckon the hunt-club dinners around Beechwood might be quite entertaining!"

"Yeah. They'd be singing, '*Doe*, a deer, a drugged-up deer …'"

"'*Ray*, a hunter with a buzz!'"

Chapter 23

Dr. Hardy had been invited by Detective Duffer to attend a specially called meeting of the Mecklenburg task force. The conference room was overflowing with officers, and the room was energized with the buzz of excited background conversation. In front of the crowded room, a young lady stood beside Ronnie Malcom. She appeared to be in her midthirties. Wearing a plain gray skirt, dark-rimmed glasses, and her hair in a bun, she had the look of a librarian.

Trooper Malcom addressed the group. "Okay. Let's get this started." The ambient noise abated. "We have a guest speaker today. This is Agent Audrey Hartman, with the FBI. She's a criminal profiler who might help us with our triple-S murder investigation. She can give us some clues that can help us recognize a serial killer."

"Thank you." Ms. Hartman spoke in a pleasant but serious tone. "As Trooper Malcom said, I do criminal profiling. Murderers who kill more than one person can be lumped into one of two categories: mass murderers or serial killers. The Virginia Tech massacre of 2007 is an example of a mass murderer. Well-known serial killers are Jack the Ripper and Ted Bundy. Both types of repetitive murderers have multiple victims but very different killing circumstances.

"Serial killers kill in patterns, usually with a cooling-off period between murders. These periods are typically four to six weeks. Supposedly, after quenching the urge to kill, the desire has to grow until it becomes strong enough to drive him to kill again."

"Our killer seems to wait four to six *months* between kills," said Detective Duffer.

"Maybe he's a little slow," commented another officer.

Once the giggling died out, Agent Hartman continued. "On the contrary," she said, "a serial killer is usually very organized. He gets some psychological gratification from killing and shows no signs of empathy. He is able to function well in society and appears as an average Joe. I use the pronoun 'he' because 90 percent of serial killers are males. They often come from childhood backgrounds of abuse, physical or sexual or both."

"Since they are largely males," said Dr. Hardy, "is there a genetic basis for this behavior?"

"Well, probably. Studies of brain functions do show some abnormalities. Killers have decreased nerve tract connections from the amygdala to the prefrontal cortex. You may well remember that the frontal lobes were the sites of lobotomies. These procedures were once done to treat insanity.

"Anyway, serial killers usually arise between the ages of thirty-five and forty-five, typically around age forty. They may exhibit sadistic or masochistic behaviors, inflicting pain and suffering on their victims."

"Our killer uses stabbings to kill," said Duffer, "and has shown sexually deviant behaviors, like sodomy."

"That's fits the profile to a T," said Hartman.

"So we're looking for a male, either black or white, around age forty," Duffer summarized. "And he may have had a history of abuse."

"That's right."

"Would he be crazy?" another officer asked.

"No, not outwardly. On the other hand, mass murderers are social misfits. They might appear *crazy*, as you called it."

Agent Hartman answered several more questions from the

eager audience. Detective Duffer's cell phone summoned him away. Hardy saw him move to the back corner to answer the call.

"Wilborne," he called out. "We gotta go!"

The two detectives made a quick exit.

It was two hours later when Dr. Hardy received a call at his home from the OCME.

"Dr. Hardy here," he answered.

"We have a ME case in the Clarksville area. Can you take it?"

"Yeah. Where is it?"

"In the lake at Occoneechee Park. Do you know where that is?"

"Yeah. I know it." It was where he frequently launched his sailboat. "Is it a drowning?"

"Probably. We don't have enough details yet."

"Okay. I'm on the way."

The August day was hot but less humid than the past two weeks. The air stood still under a blue sky, accented by a few fluffs of white clouds. At the park entrance Dr. Hardy was directed down the left road. This was in the opposite direction of the main launch ramps. He found Duffer's Crown Victoria parked near the park's east-end boat ramp. As he got out of his vehicle, Duffer walked over to meet him.

"This one's a little odd," said the detective.

"So, what's new?" Dr. Hardy responded.

Duffer continued as he led Hardy to the boat ramp. "A resident reported that he heard a boat motor running continuously. He saw this boat idling in a circle in this cove. It was empty and eventually ran aground. We searched the area and located a body."

They approached the lakeshore, where Carl Wilborne awaited in a county boat. He wore a flat, vest-type flotation device with a CO_2 cartridge inflator attached. As Duffer donned a similar vest, Wilborne handed Dr. Hardy a life jacket. It was the old standard boxy, Styrofoam-filled, bright-orange accessory.

"Gee, thanks," said Hardy halfheartedly.

"We don't usually have guests," said Wilborne. He cranked the motor and added, "Buckle up, Doc!"

The bright sunshine sparkled on the water, and the air flowing past them produced a comfortable cooling effect. Their destination was the opposite shore, across the main body of the lake. Any idle chatter was stifled by the volume of the engine.

The boat's motor grew quieter as they slowed down, approaching a red-colored clay shoreline. Duffer leaned toward Dr. Hardy and pointed.

"He's over there, against that bank," he said.

There was an object visible, bobbing in the water beside a bush. Hardy saw a blue baseball cap on top and, as they grew nearer, sunglasses still in place on the face.

"He's wearing sunglasses?" said Hardy.

"Yep. At least he's dressed up top."

"What do you mean?"

"He's got on a T-shirt but nothing from the waist down!"

Killing their engine, they drifted until the hull went aground. They were off to the side of the body, still twenty-five feet from the shoreline.

"It's pretty shallow here," said Duffer.

Hardy was glad he had on blue jeans as he removed his wallet and cell phone. Stepping out of his Top-Siders, he grabbed some blue gloves and slid over the side of the boat. As he turned toward the body, he sank up to his ankles in the mud. Thigh-deep in the water, he trudged along slowly in the soggy bottom. His movement in the water, added to the slight wake from the boat, caused the deceased to drift away from the bush. Inching into the shallower depths toward the beach, the body turned from upright to facedown. The sunglasses stayed eerily in place. Something about him reminded Hardy of the movie *Weekend at Bernie's*.

The doctor estimated the man at about sixty. He felt the hands and arms, finding rigor mortis. "He's been dead over two hours," he reported to the detectives. The body became beached in knee-deep water and stopped moving. Now the white buttocks peeked above the surface. "And I see the full moon." The vision of a nude rear end brought to his mind the recent sodomy cases. Thankfully, there was no evidence of violence here. He took an axillary temperature reading, 81.4 degrees, and then a water temperature.

"The water temperature is 78 degrees," he reported. "If he was 98.6 degrees when he died, he's been dead six to eight hours."

"Okay. Can we load him now?" asked Duffer.

"Sure."

He helped the detectives move the corpse into a nylon-mesh zippered bag. They loaded their catch into the boat and returned to Occoneechee Park.

"That's his boat on the trailer over there," said Duffer. "Todd Keefer, from Roxboro. His family reports he goes fishing for days at a time."

"Was he camping here?" said Hardy. He looked into the boat as he spoke.

"Apparently he stayed on this boat." Dr. Hardy saw rolls of toilet paper, shorts, T-shirts, and three gallon-sized bottles of bourbon, one of which was nearly empty. "We think he might have been intoxicated and lowered himself over the side to take a dump. Then he accidentally lost his grip and drowned."

"That does seem most likely. Still, with the nudity and our triple-S murders, he needs to go in for autopsy. We need to rule out any sexual assault."

"Absolutely!"

Chapter 24

Dr. Hardy was happy that his ER shift was finished on time for a change. He was on his way home by 7:20 p.m., when he called his wife, Lucy.

"I'm on the way home."

"Good," she said. "Your dog has been barking most of the day!"

"Oh yeah? What's up?"

"It seems he found a raccoon or something this morning."

"Is it dead?"

"Yeah, but he's quite proud of it."

"I'm sure," said the doctor.

"You'd better get rid of it before the buzzards start coming," she said.

"Okay. Sure. I'll see you soon."

It was near dark when Dr. Hardy reached home. A small animal carcass was clearly visible beside the front driveway. Hardy took a plastic bag from the back seat of his Jeep and approached the raccoon. He was able to slide the bag over the head and torso without touching it with his hands. He dumped it into the outdoor garbage can.

As he washed his hands afterward, he thought out loud. "You know, raccoons are our largest reservoir of rabies."

"Do you think Chase might have caught rabies?" asked Lucy.

"No, he's been vaccinated. But I think I should contact the county animal control anyway."

It was twenty minutes before Dr. Hardy received a call back from the sheriff's office.

"This is Tom Carlson, animal control."

"Yes. This is Obie Hardy. My dog has killed or found a dead raccoon. Do you monitor these critters?"

"Yep, we sure do. Did he kill it at night or daytime?" asked Carlson.

"Daytime, I guess. Why?"

"'Coons are nocturnal. If they're out during the day, it's more likely that they're rabid."

"Oh, I see."

"Where's the carcass?"

"It's in my trash can here."

"Good. I'll come and get it."

The Hardys had just finished supper when Carlson arrived. They met him outside.

"We've heard hunting dogs barking around our house at night. Do you think they're coon dogs?" asked Hardy.

"Well, legally they are," said Carlson.

"Legally?"

"To train for deer season, some deer hunters run their dogs at night. If they're caught by the game warden, they will just claim that they're coon hunting, since that is legal after sundown."

"I see. We often get stray hunting dogs wandering up in our yard."

"Hunt clubs are our rural gangs, so to speak," said Carlson.

"I hear you."

The town of Clarksville hosted an inboard speedboat competition each fall. People brought these sleek craft from across the country to showcase their speed. Watching these boats with velocities of seventy miles per hour thrilled the crowds along the lakeshore. By early October, the stifling summer swelter had eased. Most of the trees bordering the water had begun changing colors, giving red and orange highlights to the rippled surface. The smell of wood burning and simmering Brunswick stew filled the air.

Attending the event, Dr. Hardy and his wife walked along the Clarksville overlook, on the bank opposite the town. They were drawn by the rich aroma of stew cooking.

"How about some stew?" Hardy asked Lucy.

"Let's get some to take home for the girls," she said. Lucy had allergies to beef and chicken, the usual stew meats.

"Okay."

As they approached the stew pot, they found several men standing about. A tall, bearded black man with the stirring paddle was telling a story. "So, then the stew master asked the worried lady with the lost dog, 'Did it have on a purple collar?' She says 'Yeah! Did you see him?' He lifts up the paddle from the stew and chops up some of the meat chunks on it with a cleaver, shaking his head. 'I sure wish you'd have come by sooner, ma'am.' I think she 'bout fainted!"

As the other men laughed, a county deputy of medium height and stocky build approached. He looked sternly at the bearded, flannel-shirted man and spoke. "And you better watch your dogs too!" said the deputy, Ted Johnson, loudly. "You know that Cox Cove Hunt Club hunts the woods out to Beechwood Point!"

"Yeah, but your area is *south* of Lambert Creek. We hunt the *north* side," said the other man. Their voices were tainted with anger.

"If we find your dogs on our side of the creek, we won't be responsible for the circumstances!"

"Our dogs don't know where the boundary is!"

Johnson pointed a menacing finger and said, "Just let this be a warning." He glared at the man briefly before turning and walking off.

Dr. Hardy addressed the black man. "They take their hunting seriously, don't they?"

"Yeah," the man answered.

"So, do you think he'll arrest your dogs?"

"Naw. He's a bitter man. I'm afraid it would be more serious than that."

"Man, I'm sorry to hear that," said Hardy. "I would like a couple of quarts of this stew, though."

"Sure." He bagged two plastic containers and handed them to Lucy. "That'll be twelve dollars."

"Okay. Thanks."

Hardy understood the hunter's implication. A good hunting dog might bring $400 to $600. The GPS locating collars frequently used could run $700 to $800. In addition, hunting rights on properties were paid for by club dues, further raising the costs for this hobby. Venison might indeed prove to be a quite expensive meal meat. But was it worth fighting over?

Just then a pair of racing boats sped by them, just off from the overlook. The roar of the engines and splashing of the water rose to a peak as the vessels passed and then began to wane as they cruised away along the race course.

Chapter 25

Detective Duffer found Sheriff Larrimore and Ronnie Malcom standing beside his desk in an impromptu meeting of the minds.

"So, what's our plan to investigate this marijuana farm?" asked the sheriff.

"Well," said Duffer, "Tom Carlson suggested placing game cameras in the area. They're easily camouflaged and motion activated."

"That sounds good to me," said Malcom. "Do you have any of these cameras?"

"Yeah," said Larrimore. "Don't we have a couple of them, Bruce?"

"I think there're some in the back equipment room."

"All right. Let's get 'em out there."

"Okay. Good plan," said Malcom.

Bruce Duffer found two cameras in storage and commandeered some fresh batteries. He still needed two recording chips for them. He found those that afternoon at Walmart and took the cameras home that evening to prepare them for placement.

The next morning, he recruited Tom Carlson to assist him in positioning and mounting the monitors at Beechwood Point. They carried the cameras into the woods near the pot field. They discovered some wheel trails in the vicinity, which made it a likely site to record.

"The range is about fifty feet," said Carlson, "and these cameras use infrared flashes for night photos."

"Let's hope we get something useful," said Duffer.

They placed one unit near the curing barn and the other overlooking the trail.

"How often do you think we should check these?" asked Duffer.

"At least once a week. Maybe Sundays, since bow-hunting season will be opening."

"Yeah. Good point."

As they walked back to the car, Carlson looked up at the old farmhouse.

"So, Bruce, do you think the old Garner house is haunted?"

"I wouldn't doubt it. If I were a ghost, I'd hang out there."

"Well, this place has scared off buyers for generations."

"Yeah. But I think it's more sad than satanic," said Bruce. This reminded him of his work on that cold case. After the new break he had found, it seemed to have stalled again.

Upon returning to the office, Detective Duffer was met by Betsy, with a message. "Al, from JB's Car Wash, called. He said he'd found something you need to see."

"Oh yeah?" said Duffer.

"It sounded urgent," she added.

"All right. I'm on the way," said Duffer, turning back down the hall. Duffer wondered whether Al had found a clue to JB's death, although it was now closed as a suicide. Al had cleaned Duffer's Crown Vic more times than he could count. When Duffer parked at the car wash, Al came walking up, appearing anxious.

"Detective Duffer," he said. "You need to see what I've found in the garage."

"Okay. Lead on."

He followed Al into the metal building and over to a storage closet. Al opened the door, revealing some cleaning supplies and two boxes labelled Glistex.

"These boxes are full of dope!" he said, folding back the lid on one box. There were multiple bags of shredded leaves inside.

"I believe you're right, Al." Duffer put on the rubber gloves he'd brought before lifting up a sample bag. He opened it and sniffed the contents. The sweet and heady aroma of marijuana was unmistakable. "Where did this come from?"

"Some dude in a pickup brings it. I just thought it was soap."

"Do you know his name?"

"I'm not sure. JB called him Wayne, I think."

"All right. I'll look into this. If you hear from him, let me know," said the detective.

"Will do," said Al.

Detective Duffer took the two Glistex boxes of weed back to the sheriff's office. He left them in the forensics unit, where they would be dusted for prints and verified to contain pot. If JB was involved in drugs, his death might more likely have been a homicide. He returned to his office to record the general description Al had given him of the Glistex man. The suspect was a tall, heavyset, white male, probably in his midthirties. He had a dark complexion and black hair.

Suddenly, from outside of his door, Duffer heard angry voices. He heard Tom Carlson speaking. "The Lambert Creek Hunters think *you* did it!"

"Well, it wasn't me!" said Ted Johnson.

"Didn't you threaten them earlier?"

"What if I did? That doesn't mean I did anything. They need to keep their dogs off our territory!"

Detective Duffer stepped out into the hallway as Deputy Johnson stormed off.

"What's the rift?" he asked Carlson.

"The hunt clubs!" Carlson shook his head. "The Lambert Creek Hunters found one of their dogs killed. Shot in the head."

"That's awful!" said Duffer. "Where did it happen?"

"Out near Beechwood Point. The dog was found hanging from a tree along Lambert Creek."

"Jesus Christ! That's just sick!"

"Yeah. The hunt clubs with their turf battles! They're the country equivalent of the city street gangs."

"I see."

"And there are other issues as well. The Lambert Creek Hunters have mostly black members. They call the *Cox Creek Hunt Club* the KKK."

"And these guys are roaming the woods with guns!"

"Yep."

The first of the week, Duffer found himself with Tom Carlson again; they were seated in front of Duffer's computer monitor. It was certainly no home theater, but it allowed them to screen the surveillance camera photos. The photos were shot in black and white, and the image resolution was poor. They scrolled through numerous portraits of wildlife that had triggered the motion sensor—deer, dogs, coyotes. Sometimes only tree limbs swaying in the wind were visible. The viewing was tedious, despite their refreshing their coffee mugs. Finally, a vehicle popped onto the screen.

"Hey, here's something!" said Carlson. It was a pickup truck.

"Yeah, I see," said Duffer. "Try to zoom in on it."

Carlson used the mouse to toggle the image. It did enlarge but became more blurred.

"Well, for what it's worth," he said.

"Oh," said Duffer, a bit discouraged. "Well, the truck is a light color, like a tan or gray. It appears to be a Ford. Can we save that image onto a flash drive?"

"Sure."

Duffer handed him a flash drive from his desk drawer. Carlson saved the picture and forwarded to the next shot. A man was standing beside the vehicle. His facial features were indistinct.

"He appears about six feet tall," said Duffer, analyzing the image. "Dark hair, hefty size. Save this one, too."

"Sure," said Carlson. "You're very observant, Bruce. You just made a suspect description from such a blurred picture."

"It's certainly very general, but we have to start somewhere."

They downloaded a few more still shots of the truck and driver before the endless wildlife images returned. Suddenly another person appeared on the screen.

"Hey. Who's that?" said Duffer. Again, the resolution was poor, but this was obviously a different man. He was shorter and stocky.

"I think I recognize that body and posture," said Carlson. "It looks like Ted Johnson!"

Duffer studied the figure and moved to the next frame. That picture showed slightly clearer facial features.

"I believe you're right, Tom! Wonder what he would be doing out there?"

"What's the date stamp?"

"Four days ago. Why?" asked Detective Duffer.

"The camera was in Lambert Creek Hunters' territory. This was shot the day before the dog was killed."

"You think … Ted killed the dog?"

"Well, we know now he was in the area." said Carlson.

"Yeah. But even if he did, it's still just a misdemeanor."

"Unless there were repeated offenses. Then it could reach felony status. I've heard it said that anyone who could kill a dog could kill a child."

Duffer pondered in silence. Could this type of cruelty be powerful enough to make someone the triple-S killer? He suddenly remembered Deputy Johnson's behavior while they'd been searching for JB's vehicle—and Skylar had listened to this man too.

"Uh-huh," was Duffer's subdued response.

Chapter 26

The polling site in Boydton was the county school board building. Few residents would remember that it had been the cafeteria building for the long-since-abandoned elementary school campus. Lining the street out front, people stood alongside of campaign posters. Both of the candidates for sheriff were present this morning. Bruce Duffer was stopping in on his way to work to cast his vote. He smiled and waved at both Skylar Daniels and Ronnie Malcom. One of these men would become his boss. He dared not show any favoritism, even though he hoped in his heart that Ronnie would win.

Inside the building, he found Dr. Hardy and his wife among the voters.

"They let just anybody vote here, I see," said Dr. Hardy.

"Yeah. That's just what I was thinking," said Duffer, smiling.

"Oh, Bruce," said the doctor. "Did you hear anymore from the ME's office on the man we pulled from the lake?"

"Well ..." He looked around them before answering. "He most likely doesn't fit the pattern. It's not definite yet, so not ruled out, either."

Dr. Hardy nodded that he understood and did not press for any details. It was a public place.

"Okay," said Hardy. "Thanks."

"We voted for Ronnie!" Lucy whispered to the detective as they walked off.

When Duffer arrived at his office, Betsy handed him a printout. "Bruce, here's the breakdown you requested."

"Thanks," said Duffer. He had asked that she run a list of all Ford pickup trucks registered in Mecklenburg County. She was to exclude all white and dark-colored ones—black, red, or blue. This narrowed the field down to 482 vehicles. Duffer began pulling up driver's license photos and scrolling through them, comparing each to the field-camera images. Most were easily eliminated— fat, short, female, non-Caucasian. Others were not so obvious. He kept many of these in the lineup. After about two hours, he had narrowed the list down to thirty-seven possible suspects. It was time for a break.

He needed Al to review his suspect candidates. Heading out of the office to the car wash, Duffer met Ted Johnson as he pulled up into the parking lot. He was driving his SUV and quickly hopped out.

"Hey, Bruce," he greeted.

"Are you off today?" asked Duffer.

"Yeah. Going fishing. I just left my cooler here at the office."

"Okay. Good luck."

As Johnson hurried into the office, Duffer glanced over into the back of his SUV. One of the fishing rods caught his eye. It was a burgundy-colored, moderate-weight rod with an open-face reel. What had drawn him to it was a band of white duct tape about two feet above the reel. Something seemed very familiar about that feature.

He found Al at JB's and recruited him to review the DMV photos. Al seemed eager to help and rode with him back to the sheriff's office. He showed Al the surveillance shots of the suspect.

"Does this look like the Glistex salesman and his truck?" asked Duffer.

"Well, this isn't that clear, but it sure looks like him."

"Fair enough." Duffer pulled up his DMV photos next. "If

any of these photos look like him, let me know. Even if you're not sure, pick any that even resemble him."

"Okay, sure."

They flipped through the images, one by one. After about twenty shots with a couple of "maybes," Al suddenly sat up straight.

"That's him! I'm pretty sure that's him!" Al pointed excitedly at the computer screen.

"Wayne Dodson," Duffer read from the ID. "Okay. Let's just go through the rest of them to be sure that there are no other possibilities."

"Okay, yeah."

The remaining pictures produced only one more possibility. Duffer returned Al to the car wash before continuing his work. He compared the addresses of the subject with the other three possibilities. Wayne Dodson lived in Palmer Springs, about two miles from Beechwood Point! This should be enough for a search warrant.

Ted's fishing rod, however, was still gnawing away at him. Where had he seen it before? Could it be from one of the fisherman murders?

"Betsy," he spoke into the speaker phone.

"Yes?"

"Can you pull the file on the Ralph Forman murder for me?"

"Sure."

He had the file in minutes and immediately took out the pictures. The Forman family had given him some photos to help with identifying any stolen property. One photo showed Forman holding up a large striper in one hand and a fishing pole in the other. It was a burgundy rod with a band of white tape. When he had asked the family about the tape, they'd told him most of his rods were wrapped like that. The holding rack in his truck bed fit the handles well, but the rods were thinner. He had added tape to the shafts to help hold them more snugly.

What the hell! he said to himself. First Ted had harassed JB and obstructed his death investigation. Next, it looked as if he had killed a hunting dog. Now this fishing rod was connecting him to the triple-S murders. Could Ted Johnson, a Mecklenburg County deputy, be such a heinous villain?

Detective Duffer stood up and carried the photo to Sheriff Larrimore's office. He found Carl Wilborne in the office with the sheriff. Duffer quietly closed the door and spoke softly to the two of them.

"This is of photo of Ralph Forman's fishing gear. This rod was reported missing from that truck parked at the dam."

"Oh yeah," said Wilborne. "I remember that."

"Well, I'm pretty sure Ted Johnson has this rod. I saw it in the back of his SUV today. It's this same rod."

"Why are you so sure?" asked Clay Larrimore.

"The white duct tape." He pointed to the photo. "He taped his rods to fit tight in his truck rack!"

Larrimore and Wilborne studied the photo in silence. The gravity of this discovery was disquieting.

"It sounds too far off to be a coincidence," said Larrimore.

"Well," said Wilborne. "I could try to get him to tell me where he got it. Maybe he won't realize we're suspicious of anything."

"Okay. That sounds good," said Larrimore. "We don't want to jump to any conclusions."

"Yeah," said Duffer. "Maybe you can find out something that way." It seemed better than targeting him or getting a search warrant.

"All right," said Wilborne.

"Oh, on a lesser note," said Duffer, "I may have ID'd our pot farmer."

"Oh yeah?" said Larrimore. "What have you got?"

"I've matched a truck owner with a witness ID to a Wayne Dodson, thirty-six-year-old male. And, get this, he lives in Palmer Springs, two miles from Beechwood Point!"

"Sounds like our perp," said Wilborne.

"So, you need a warrant, huh?" said Larrimore.

"Yeah. I've got the papers filled out. I'm thinking we can take a team out there tomorrow."

"Okay, you've got it," said Larrimore. "And good work, detective!"

Chapter 27

Wednesday morning found Duffer arriving early at the sheriff's office. He walked past Carl Wilborne, hovering inside the entrance. Carl was on the lookout for Ted Johnson. When Ted entered the office, Carl approached him and started a friendly conversation.

"Any luck fishing, Ted?" he asked.

"Not bad," said Ted. "Do you fish?"

"Yeah, some. Hey, I was wondering, where's a good place to buy fishing gear?"

"Well, it depends. You can get your basic stuff, say, at Walmart. And Bobcat's, in Clarksville, has a lot of tackle geared for our lake."

"Okay. Sounds good."

"But," Ted said, smiling brightly, "I've found some great buys at pawn shops. Especially Mack's Pawn in Norlina."

"Great! Thanks, Ted."

Betsy, Duffer's assistant, stepped out into the hallway and addressed the pair. "Sheriff Larrimore's called a morning muster meeting. It's at 7:45, conference room 2."

"Okay," said Wilborne. "Thanks."

Duffer found Sheriff Larrimore standing in the front of the conference room as he gathered with his fellow officers. The sheriff then addressed them over their mumbling and coffee sipping. "All right, men, settle down. Let's get started."

As the room grew quiet, someone called out, "Who won the election?"

"They haven't announced it yet. A computer problem in Chase City has slowed down the final count. We'll know later today.

"Anyway, we're here this morning to form a team. We've ID'd a local marijuana dealer and have issued a search warrant. We need a team of at least four officers to work the search. Bruce Duffer will be the lead investigator. Do we have any volunteers?"

An array of hands arose.

"Bruce. Pick your team."

Duffer noted that Ted Johnson's hand was among those raised. He remembered the problems with JB's site search and weighed that against his rising suspicions now. Maybe including him would allow Duffer to maintain close personal surveillance.

"Ted," he said on his fifth and final pick, pointing to Deputy Johnson.

"Anything on the triple-S murders?" asked another deputy.

"Well, we may have found a soft lead, but I can't elaborate at this time," said the sheriff. "Anyway, thanks for your time and service. And remember to serve and protect."

As the officers were dispersing, Wilborne approached Duffer. He was one of Duffer's six-membered search team. "Bruce, I've got something to check out. Something from that file photo."

Bruce sensed an eagerness from Carl. "Okay. Do you need to drop off the team?"

"No," he said. "But I'll need to continue on to Norlina while you start the search. I can catch up to you there later."

"Okay," said Duffer.

Wilborne smiled slyly. "And you'll be keeping an eye on Ted, then?"

"Absolutely!" replied Duffer. He was glad now that he had chosen Ted. He announced loudly, "Search team! Meet in the rear parking lot in fifteen minutes!"

Detective Duffer assembled the search team beside the Mecklenburg Crime Unit van in the parking area. "We'll take the van and three cruisers. Skylar, you can drive the van. Ted can ride with me. Carl, you'll be solo." That way Carl would be free to leave for his recon.

The unit pulled out in tandem, convoy style, with the van closing the rear. As they rolled past Beechwood Point, Duffer spoke to Ted, whom he knew to be a hunting fanatic. "So, do you think there'll be plenty of deer this season?"

"I hope so. Bow season opens this Saturday."

"Did you know that deer would eat marijuana?"

"I hadn't much thought about it, but I guess it makes sense."

They turned onto Palmer Springs Trail and reached Wayne Dodson's address shortly. His truck was not in the dirt driveway. The warrant was to search the premises and his vehicle for suspected drugs. They parked in front of the house, and Duffer led the team to the door.

The residence was a small clapboard house. It had once been painted white, but it now appeared grayish from aging paint and exposed wood siding. The window trim was black. Out back there was a shed with tin siding. Duffer banged on the door three times before taping the search warrant beside the door and ordering the team to ram open the door.

The door swung open on the second thrust, and Duffer yelled into the house, "Wayne Dodson! Mecklenburg Sheriff's Office! We have a warrant!"

The house was vacant. The team walked into the den. On one wall, two framed plaques were mounted displaying arrowheads and stone tool fragments. There was a cardboard box on a nearby table containing more irregularly shaped rock objects.

"Wow at the arrowheads!" said Skylar as he donned his rubber gloves.

"Actually, they're projectile points," said Duffer.

Carl approached Duffer, carrying his camera, and announced, "Oh, crap! I've got to go get some batteries and a data card."

"Okay. But hurry back," said Duffer, validating the alibi.

"Sure thing."

"Bruce," called Skylar from the next room. "You gotta see this!"

Bruce stepped into the adjoining bedroom. The dresser top was covered with knives. There were many sizes and styles, from pocket knives, to buck-skinning knives, to wilderness-survival knives.

"Holy crap!" exclaimed Bruce. "He certainly likes knives!"

Duffer had begun photographing the array of weapons when Johnson's voice from another room interrupted him. "Guys. His main arsenal is in here!"

Duffer and Skylar promptly stepped through the next doorway to find an apparent office, with a small desk and chair. In one corner there was a tall wooden gun cabinet with glass doors. Visible inside were four shotguns, three handguns, and a .30-06 scoped rifle. Boxes of ammunition were stacked in the bottom of the case.

Duffer let out a low-pitched whistle. "He's ready for his own war here!"

Just then the sound of a vehicle engine outside drew Duffer to the window. He saw a bronze-colored pickup driving up. He rushed out the front door as a tall, dark-haired man got out of the truck.

"Hey! What the hell's going on here?" the man bellowed.

"Wayne Dodson?" Duffer said.

"Yeah?"

"I'm Detective Duffer from the Mecklenburg Sheriff's Office. We have a warrant to search these premises and your vehicle for evidence of drug possession and trafficking."

"What? You're trespassing! You busted my door?" he cried out, angrily.

"You can cooperate with us or we can arrest you for obstruction of justice, failing to comply with a search warrant."

"Goddammit! This is a violation! I'll sue your asses!"

"Mr. Dodson, we found some firearms here. Are they registered to you?"

"I ain't saying shit to you assholes!"

"Skylar," called Bruce. "Search his truck!"

Skylar Daniels opened the driver's door of Dodson's truck. A cardboard box was on the seat, and Skylar looked inside it. "Bingo!" he exclaimed. He held up a plastic bag of crushed leaves.

"Wayne Dodson," intoned Detective Duffer, "you're under arrest for possession of marijuana with intent to distribute."

"This is bullshit!" Dodson cried out as Duffer cuffed him.

"Ted," said Duffer. "Take him in and process him while we finish the search."

"All right, Bruce," he answered. "This way, Dodson."

"Skylar, let's check out the shed in the back."

"Okay. I'll get the bolt cutters out just in case."

They did, indeed, need the cutters to snap open the padlock on the shed door. Inside the tin structure there was a stale, heady, somewhat herbal odor. A countertop was strewn with uncrushed, dried marijuana leaves. Stacked beside this were several pasteboard boxes, like the one in the truck, with Glistex inscribed on the sides. Some were filled with baggies of dried marijuana leaves.

"I guess he brought his dried and cured leaves in here," said Duffer.

"Looks like it," Skylar agreed.

As Duffer photographed the weed, Skylar discovered a white metal box and tugged at the lid.

"This looks like a tool box for a pickup truck bed," said Skylar. "And it's padlocked, too."

Duffer took a couple of shots at the box and then said, "Okay. You can cut this lock off too."

As Skylar wrestled with the bolt cutters, Duffer's cell phone rang.

"Bruce!" said Carl Wilborne's voice.

"Yeah?" he answered.

"I've got some bad news. We may need to stop the search for now."

"Really? What's up?" said Duffer.

The steel lock popped off, and Skylar clanked open the lid of the toolbox. A faint scent of dead animal arose, and Skylar exclaimed, "Oh my God!"

Chapter 28

Dr. Hardy was awakened by his cell phone buzzing at one forty-five in the afternoon. He was working night shifts this week and would usually not arise until four. His mind was dulled by this intrusion into his slumber. "Dr. Hardy here," he muttered.

"This is the 911 office. Can you do a scene visit for an ME case?"

"Yeah, I guess so. Where is it?"

"Out past Beechwood Point, on Palmer Springs Trail."

"Okay. Give me twenty minutes."

He didn't bother shaving. There should be time for that later, before his shift started. As he walked out to his Jeep, the cool air struck his face, helping to awaken him. By two o'clock he was driving across the dam. The afternoon sun sparkled on the lake's surface. He easily found the address on Palmer Springs Trail, as it was marked, as usual, by police cars and the crime unit van.

Detective Duffer met Hardy as he parked out in front. "We discovered something that may be human remains," said the detective. He led Dr. Hardy to the shed behind Dodson's house. Hardy's curiosity was stirred. They entered the shed while Wilborne and Skylar stood at the doorway. Duffer handed Hardy some gloves.

"It's in the box," said Duffer, lifting the lid of the box.

Hardy noted two irregularly circular-shaped, hairy, flat objects, like road-kill animals. He got a whiff of the decayed flesh smell. "Are these ... scalps?" Dr. Hardy queried aloud.

"That's what we're suspecting," said Duffer.

"I can't tell you for sure that they're human," said Dr. Hardy. "I've never seen scalps before! But if these are scalps, there is readable DNA here."

"So, if these are from the triple-S murders, we can match them to the bodies."

"Yes! I guess we send them to the ME's office for processing." He had never sent body parts for postmortem examination before, especially from two probably different bodies. "We need to bag them separately, paper bags if we have them."

"Yes, we have them," said Duffer. He sent Skylar to fetch them. "Doc, we were searching the premises for drugs when Investigator Wilborne called me. Apparently this dude has been selling fishing equipment that was Ralph Forman's, the body they found in Manson."

"He's hocked a lot of other stuff, too," added Wilborne. "Sometimes, he would just make trades, usually for knives or guns."

"There's a shitload of weapons in the house," said Duffer.

Skylar walked up with the bags. "Thanks," said Hardy. He wondered how he would complete the CME-1 forms, or even if he needed to. One form or two? "How do we label them?"

"I photographed them as they were found and marked them as *A* and *B*," said Duffer.

"Great. We'll mark the bags accordingly." With the specimens removed, Dr. Hardy noticed some other items in the box. "Hey, what's this stuff?"

"It's just some old necklaces and junk," said Duffer.

Something about the jewels seemed familiar to Dr. Hardy. There were necklaces with coins attached, a crucifix medallion, a hair comb, and a wide silver ring with floral and leaf patterns.

"This looks like jewelry from the Samuel Goode graveyard by the lake," said Dr. Hardy.

"Where we found the first scalping?" asked Duffer.

"Yeah. Betty Tanner had all the relocated remains laid out in a warehouse. Many of the graves had this style of jewelry buried with the bodies."

"No shit?" said Duffer. "This is looking even more like our guy! I'll call Ms. Tanner and see if someone can verify that these jewels are a match."

"Yeah," said Hardy. "And maybe she can transport our 'bodies' to the Richmond office."

Chapter 29

Detective Duffer brought Ronnie Malcom with him to the commonwealth attorney's office. It was on Washington Street, across from the county courthouse. Charles Whitaker currently held the position as prosecutor of felony crimes in Virginia. His gray hair gave him a seasoned look. He studied the report that Duffer had delivered personally. Duffer was presenting his evidence against Wayne Dodson and seeking an indictment.

"So, this looks like solid evidence against Dodson," said Whitaker, peering through his wire-framed reading glasses. "Now, how was it obtained?"

"The search warrant," said Duffer. He handed Whitaker a copy from his folder.

"Okay," said the commonwealth attorney. Reading the paper, he continued. "It says 'for evidence of drug possession and distribution.' Where were the scalps and jewelry found?"

"In the shed behind the house," said Duffer.

"Was the shed open?"

"Well, there was a padlock on the door."

"Oh. And were they lying about inside?"

"No," Duffer said, hesitatingly. He knew where these questions were leading. Whitaker was assuring the discoveries would not be discredited. "They were in a metal tool box."

"Was the lid open?"

"It was padlocked too."

The commonwealth attorney paused pensively before

continuing. He reread the document as if the wording might have changed. The atmosphere grew heavy.

"You know that with a search warrant for drugs, any additional criminal evidence is only discoverable if it is readily visible, out in the open. The scalps and jewelry were securely hidden, protected with two padlocks. Sadly, their procurement is considered the result of an illegal search."

"So ..." said Duffer.

"They are inadmissible as evidence," Whitaker said flatly.

"Damn!" exclaimed Duffer.

"So this monster gets off? He gets away with murder?" demanded Ronnie Malcom.

"I'm afraid so. Just like OJ Simpson. Unless ..."

"Unless what?" said Malcom.

"Unless you can find some additional evidence to build a case."

Malcom appeared to be in deep thought as he rubbed his chin with his hand.

It seemed like no time before Detective Duffer was standing in the courtroom before the county judge. Wayne Dodson stood off to his left.

"Wayne Dodson," stated the judge, "you're charged with possession and distribution of marijuana and possession of unlicensed firearms. How do you plead to these charges?"

"Not guilty, Your Honor," he answered smugly.

"And to the charges of possession of unregistered firearms?"

"Not guilty, Your Honor."

"Okay. You have a court date scheduled January twelfth. Bail is set at fifteen hundred dollars."

"Thank you, Your Honor."

Duffer struggled to restrain his anger, even as Dodson smirked at him while he was being led away. Duffer approached the judge's bench. "I'll be back with evidence of more charges."

"I hope so, Detective. I sincerely do."

Returning to the sheriff's office, Duffer found it electrified with some breaking news. The official vote counts were finally in. The new Mecklenburg County sheriff would be Ronnie Malcom. Duffer was pleased, and he sensed that most of the department was as well. He retreated to his desk with this glimmer of hope beneath his cloud of despair. This Dodson devil was undoubtedly the triple-S killer, and he was now out on bail for a marijuana and weapons charge. He would need to do something fast. Dodson was wise to the police now, probably laughing, knowing they were powerless. There had to be another way!

Chapter 30

Monday morning, after a week of midnight shifts, Dr. Hardy slept until noon. He arose then for the remainder of his hangover day. He was rubbing the sleep from his eyes when he found Lucy at the kitchen island.

"You gotta read this!" she said excitedly, handing him the *News Progress* paper.

"Triple-S Serial Killer Arrested in NC," read the headline, immediately jarring Dr. Hardy awake. "Wow! This is great news!"

"Apparently," said Lucy, "they linked him to that body they found in Manson."

"So that's why North Carolina got him," said Hardy. "I thought Duffer would have arrested him." They had found all that evidence at his house. He wondered how things had changed. The body that he'd been charged for had nonetheless been found in North Carolina.

"It says that, earlier, Mecklenburg charged him with drugs and firearms and released him on bail."

"Oh, okay."

"Did you know that man was scalped? They initially just reported some mutilation to the body."

"Yeah. It was a detail they needed to withhold so as not to jeopardize the investigation."

"I see," she said. "So, do you think Detective Duffer might be free now to investigate the ghost cat?"

At the sheriff's office, Detective Duffer was at his desk with Carl Wilborne, reading the story as well.

"I'm glad Warren County could act so quickly," said Wilborne.

"Well, it was their case anyway," said Duffer. He felt a bit cheated, still, knowing his work had been instrumental to the case.

"Yeah. As soon as I gave them the pawn shop info, they took it and ran."

"I was afraid that removing the scalps from the residence would jeopardize their investigation," said Duffer.

"I know. But there were enough loose hairs in the toolbox to make a DNA match with Forman's body. We lucked out on that one!"

Larrimore and Sheriff-elect Ronnie Malcom walked into Duffer's office looking cheerful. "You guys basking in the glory of your headlines?" asked Larrimore.

"Kind of," said Duffer.

"We cherish the few victories we have around here," said Wilborne.

"Well, I hope you don't get too excited about this, then. It seems our sheriff-elect here, Ronnie, did some more work on your killer," said Larrimore.

"What do you mean?" asked Duffer.

"Ronnie, here, pulled the feds in on this!"

"The FBI?" said Wilborne.

"Yeah," said Ronnie slyly. "The FBI was able to find some scalp follicles ID'd as Victor Soloman's."

"The graveyard burial case," said Duffer.

"Yeah. And the pawn shop still had some of that Yugoslavian jewelry that he reported was hocked by Dodson. They're going to charge him with that murder, as well!"

"No kidding?" said Duffer excitedly. "That's incredible!"

"And?" said Larrimore. He smiled at Ronnie.

"And … when they processed Dodson's DNA swab, it matched to one of the Texas murder cases," said Ronnie.

"Seems he spent a couple of years in Texas before moving back here," sheriff Larrimore added.

"They'll extradite him to Texas once we're done with him," said Ronnie Malcom. "And, Texas still has the death penalty!"

"And they make good use of it!" added Larrimore.

Chapter 31

"Bruce," Betsy's voice came over the speakerphone. "Mark Malone is here to see you."

"Okay, send him in," said Bruce. The reporter from the *News Progress* probably wanted the weekly police files update. A tall, slender black man with a wide grin approached his desk.

"The famous Detective Duffer," Malone said.

"It's just Bruce, Mark. Have a seat."

"Okay, thanks."

"Not much exciting this week, just what you got from the courthouse, I guess. The triple-S murderer is still awaiting trial in North Carolina."

"Yeah. But I hear you've got something else exciting now."

"I'm not sure what you mean."

"The local legend! The Garner murders!"

"Oh, that," said Duffer. He hadn't thought that cold case would draw much attention. "Yeah. We finally closed it."

"Well, tell me about it." Malone produced a miniature Dictaphone recorder and clicked it on.

"All right. It all hinged on sending a handkerchief from the scene for DNA testing. We got a speculative relative match from CODIS. What was incredible was that the match was also that of the triple-S killer suspect, Wayne Dodson."

"But he wasn't even born at the time of the murders," said Malone. He was attempting to make sense of the story.

"True. But the relative match meant that he was a second-degree relative of the killer. Dodson's father died while he was young, and he was raised by his alcoholic uncle. His grandfather was unstable. He had some minor brushes with the law. He lost the family farm to eminent domain during construction of the lake reservoir. After he squandered the buyout money, he left the area, moving to Texas. That's where he died. Wayne Dodson probably went to Texas to settle his grandfather's affairs."

"So it was Dodson's grandfather who was the Garner murderer?"

"Yep. Harold Dodson."

"And you found all this out from a booger?"

"Yeah." Duffer replied and laughed.

"I guess the apple doesn't fall far from the tree."

"That's true here—and a wormy apple at that!" He stood up from his desk. "Now, I'm going to play at a bluegrass gig this afternoon."

The *News Progress*'s next edition had a headline that read: "County Cracks Cold Case: Legendary Garner Murders Linked to Triple-S Killer."

Dr. Hardy, ME

Elemental Danger
Episode Two

It was a pleasant, sunny May afternoon in rural Virginia. Since it was Wednesday, Dr. Obie Hardy was finishing his office work early, planning to enjoy his yard and grill some hamburgers. For over two decades he had practiced family medicine in the small town of Boydton. As he dropped a final stack of office charts on the refile counter, his medical assistant, Lorene, spoke. "The sheriff's office needs a medical examiner," she said.

"Great," said Dr. Hardy with a sigh.

"They're on line one," she added.

"Dr. Hardy," he acknowledged as he hit the speakerphone button. All of his patients were gone for the day, so the discussion would still be private.

"Yes. We need an ME on Route 722, Buffalo Springs area, near the Halifax County line." Dr. Hardy realized that this was at least twenty miles one way. A typical death-scene visit took him over an hour to work. It might be dark by the time he got home now. "It's on the lakeshore," the caller continued.

"Okay. I'm on the way."

Dr. Hardy was one of the five doctors in Mecklenburg County who served as local medical examiners, or coroners. They worked fatality cases as extensions of the central office into their rural community, which was a hundred miles from Richmond. Local MEs received a small per-case stipend for collecting the necessary information and specimens of body fluids, if needed. He grabbed his nylon ME bag, stocked with state forms and collection supplies, and headed west on Highway 58.

The tortuous drive down back roads took him past Buffalo Springs to a somewhat geographically isolated region along the southern banks of Buggs Island Lake. A Mecklenburg County police cruiser parked beside a cabin marked the site for Dr. Hardy.

An overweight uniformed deputy met Dr. Hardy at the cabin. "Dr. Hardy, I'll take you from here to the scene. It's a couple hundred yards back this way," he said, indicating. He led Hardy along a steep path down from a bluff behind the cabin. The vivid blue water spread out below them as soft mounds of white clouds rolled slowly through the sky above. There was a bridge visible far down the lake, and Dr. Hardy realized it was the train trestle at Clarksville, at least five miles away.

The path ended on a beach of tan-colored sand with four- to eight-foot-tall brushy trees scattered about.

The deputy pointed. "There's Detective Duffer over there." He sounded a little winded.

"Thanks."

Bruce Duffer was a few years younger than Hardy, probably about fifty. This capable Mecklenburg County detective was seasoned by twenty years of experience. He was about six feet tall, with brown hair, and he was wearing a dress-type shirt and khakis. He looked over at Hardy. "Dr. Hardy. We found these remains over here."

Hardy approached cautiously, expecting a waterlogged corpse, wet and decayed. "The remains are all skeletal," Duffer announced, gesturing toward the wooded area up the beach. "We've marked and photographed the bones up front. You can check those first."

Hardy walked toward the first marker, where he found a large bone. He identified it as a left femur or thigh bone. He marveled at the pristine condition of the bone, a welcome change from the fetid, rotting bodies often encountered by MEs. Detective Duffer had brought a large brown paper bag, like a shopping bag.

"Left femur," he announced, carefully depositing it into the bag. The bone was white and dry; no adherent organic material remained. The next skeletal element marked was a pelvis. "This is a male," concluded Dr. Hardy.

"Are you sure?" probed the overweight deputy, Johnson.

"Yeah," he said. "Definitely."

"Well, there's a female missing person from Halifax County. She's been lost about three months. People said she was kinda manly, not very feminine. Could this be her?"

"No, it's a male pelvis," remarked Hardy. "And besides, these bones have been here over six months." The sand, sun, and weather had cleaned and bleached this skeleton to the quality of an anatomic teaching model.

"Any idea how old he was?" asked Duffer. Hardy had just harvested another bone sample, a portion of the lumbar spine. Five vertebrae were fused with calcified, hardened growth connecting them. This was an arthritic process that would not be seen in a young adult.

"Over thirty," stated Hardy. "Probably fifty or sixty." The osteoporosis seen in more advanced age was not present. As they proceeded inland to the woods, they found that the bones were more scattered—a couple of hand bones, some ribs, a clavicle, and so on. Dr. Hardy began losing track of which bones had been recovered. "Bruce," he said, noting that he was holding additional bags. "Can we sort the bags for different body parts?"

"Sure. How many do you need?"

"Upper extremities, lower extremities, spine and pelvis, ribs, and head. Four or five, I guess."

"No problem. Just tell me how you want to label them."

"Okay. We'll put these vertebrae in with the pelvis. Label it Spine and Pelvis."

Recovery became more difficult as they entered the edge of the woods. Ribs and long bones blended in with the branches and twigs on the ground, being partially buried in sandy soil and leaves. The time intervals between bone findings grew longer as the daylight waned. The dusk seemed to be falling early.

"We'll have to come back tomorrow," said Detective Duffer. "The storm's almost here!"

Dr. Hardy had been engrossed in completing the skeletal puzzle, unaware of the ominous dark clouds approaching. He suddenly realized that the wind was whipping up.

"Let's get these bones to the van," directed Duffer. He had the area yellow-taped off and had methodically laid out a grid, plotting the coordinates of each bone. His arduous labor could be eradicated by a heavy storm. Dr. Hardy led the ascent along the path, followed by Deputy Johnson carrying the bone bags and, lastly, Detective Duffer.

The tan-colored van with Mecklenburg County Crime Scene Unit painted on it was parked near the cottage. As Duffer placed the bones inside, the first raindrops began falling.

"I noticed," he remarked, "there were no signs of clothing. No shoes, belt buckles, jewelry, or purse fragments. Either this person was nude or moved from the site of death. You would expect some clothing remnants to persist. You know—zippers, buttons, or something."

"Yeah. I would think so too," responded Hardy.

"I'll come back tomorrow with a metal detector and sift the sand for trace evidence."

"Okay. I'll send my preliminary report to the Richmond office." The rain began to intensify, and the group dispersed to their vehicles. Dr. Hardy called his wife on the drive home and offered to pick up pizza, the backyard barbecue plan having been spoiled. He could complete the CME-1 form after supper.

"That's fine," replied his wife, Lucy. "I'll make us salads and some tea."

Other books by Willoughby Hundley III, MD

M-81 Emerging Doctors

Dr. Hardy, ME

Ashes of Deception
Episode one

Elemental Danger
Episode two

Evil Wake
Episode three

Hundleybooks.com

Printed in the United States
By Bookmasters